"Page turning suspense, Seán writes with an ease of pen rarely seen. The most beautifully terrifying birth you've ever read. It haunted me for days."

Bo Sejer
Author of *To Those Who Are Asleep*

"A truly gripping tale, Seán sets up an enthralling series of events that will bring out the fear in anyone with a heartbeat. This story will pull you along on a gruelling ride as a young pregnant woman is pitted against all the odds. You won't want to put this book down."

Barry Keegan
Author of *The Bog Road*

To Ursla,

Thank you very much for buying my book! I hope you enjoy it!!

THE MONGREL

Seán O'Connor

Matador
9 Priory Business Park,
Wistow Road, Kibworth Beauchamp,
Leicestershire. LE8 0RX
Tel: 0116 279 2299
Email: books@troubador.co.uk
Web: www.troubador.co.uk/matador
Twitter: @matadorbooks

Paperback ISBN 978 1789015 447
Hardback ISBN 978 1789015 454

British Library Cataloguing in Publication Data.
A catalogue record for this book is available from the British Library.

Printed and bound in Great Britain by 4edge Limited
Typeset in 11pt Bookman Old Style by Troubador Publishing Ltd, Leicester, UK

Matador is an imprint of Troubador Publishing Ltd

For Orla

"No one but a woman can help a man when he is in trouble of the heart."

Bram Stoker

PART ONE

ONE

Under a full moon, man can be driven to lunacy and lovers swoon with lust, but for those who breathe beneath the celestial body, menacing unease and worry can pollute the mind. This can lead to the smallest detail being missed, which, in turn, can create the world's biggest problems, sometimes out of nothing. But maybe the problem was there all along, just waiting to happen. This was the harsh life-lesson Erin Greene would soon come to learn, as the small rural town of Lusk, off to the north of Dublin, prepared itself for yet another cold winter.

The met office had issued a status-orange national weather warning, with a possible upgrade to red and a heavy snow from the east predicted before nightfall, but Erin refused to believe this as she gazed out from the balcony of her apartment. She lifted her face to the warmth of an Indian summer's breeze, its gentle caress a sharp contrast to the burning anxiety prickling her gut. Something deep inside had been niggling at her all morning, but she couldn't grasp its significance, which worried her even more.

She chewed at a nail, a habit she'd taken to in times of stress, and one her father had always given out to her about. And these were stressful times. Her reflection in the balcony window confirmed this, and she hated what she saw. Her big blue eyes, still edged by yesterday's make-up, were beyond tired, sunken behind shadowed bags. She'd have to do something with her hair, too, stuck for too long in a messy bun, neglected and unwashed. Never one for keeping up a glamorous appearance, she did, however, like to maintain a certain standard—which usually resembled an alternative, rocker look.

Her father would go ballistic if he saw the state of her, wandering around and chewing away on her fingers, wearing a pair of dark-blue maternity jeans and an oversized and over-washed black hoodie. It wasn't her fault, though, and she wasn't always like this. When her mind was clear, she excelled in everything she focused on—both productivity in work and creativity in her hobbies would be high, and her drive to succeed fuelled a sense of positive self-worth and pride. However, the waves that moved her thoughts had a habit of shifting in violent swells, and sometimes it got so bad she was like a passenger on a rudderless ship caught in a storm. At its worst, she was stranded under the weight of worry, often drifting in and out of a zombie-like daydream. Sometimes, it was the escape she needed, but not always.

She smiled up as the afternoon sun peeked out from behind a cream-colored cloud meandering across an otherwise clear-blue sky. Hard to believe winter was bearing down on them, but at least the skies were mostly clear for the full moon tonight. The town had a small but growing population—many locals debated whether it was a town or simply a large village. Either way, it was miles from her family home back on the Southside of Dublin. At first, she'd enjoyed the slower pace of life and the quiet surroundings, but it didn't take long for the isolation to creep in, and once it did, she struggled to adapt.

Something smashing inside snapped her away from her temporary bliss. Hopefully it wasn't one of her mother's vintage plates—there weren't too many left, and she feared for the remainder now that Philip's rage was in full swing again.

"I'm sick and tired of it, Erin!" he screamed out at her, his thick voice booming. "What the fuck are we even doing in this shit place? We're miles away from everything."

She clasped her hands and closed her eyes. He knew the reason they chose Lusk, just as well as she did. Money, and their lack of it. Rents in the city had spiralled so high, they'd been priced out of all desirable areas, and with their baby due in almost a month, they needed an affordable place to live at short notice, and so they'd settled on the small two-bed apartment off to the north of Dublin.

The interior was a boring magnolia and, much to her dismay, the landlord had insisted that it couldn't be changed. The furniture had seen better days, but at the same time carried a certain old-world charm. The wooden floors were worn and full of scratches, and tenants were only allowed hang pictures in designated places. Along with their personal belongings, the cutlery in the kitchen and the television were the only items that didn't belong to the owner.

"Shut up, Phil, will you?" she snapped back at him, his groans getting right into her head. "Please." That came as a frightened whimper when she realised she'd actually spoken aloud.

She cradled her large bump in an attempt to shield the baby from witnessing the unfolding argument, but she was in no doubt the poor thing could sense the tension, what with it kicking like a mad thing against her ribs.

While he ranted away inside, she turned and looked over the balcony rail, happy to give out to him out of earshot. "You've done nothing but complain since we moved here. If we could afford to stay in the city, then we would have."

Silence. Did he hear her? She coughed out the lump of fearful apprehension. They'd fought worse than ever since the move—so much she didn't have the energy to fight anymore.

"Fuck it, Erin, I should've took that job-offer in Canada. We could be well set up by now and I'd be earning some real money. Just like Geoff." The whine had increased in his voice, the French hues colouring his Southside brogue, as always happened when he was about to lose it. She glanced inside to see where he was, glimpsing him pacing through their small kitchen.

She was used to him losing it. Her man, Philip Montague, tall and handsome. He enjoyed exploiting his height, towering over her five-feet-two. It had attracted her at first, before she learned that he thought it gave him the right to dominate anyone smaller than him. He kept his hair short and neat, especially now that he was pretty much bald on top, making up for it by way of a fully-grown beard. His friends in Dublin sometimes called him *Monti the Monster,* as he cut an intimidating figure and would often be the one to settle physical altercations when out on the rip.

He could always be found in a black skin-tight t-shirt, the short sleeves hugging his biceps. His wardrobe didn't feature much other than black jeans, t-shirts, and leather jackets. She knew he missed his friends and the social scene in Dublin, especially his best friend—and doppelganger—Geoff Baron, who'd emigrated to Canada a few months ago and by all accounts was doing very well for himself, though it rankled Phil bigtime that he'd stopped phoning him and seemed to have just slipped off the grid. He was a jealous man, which he made no secret about, and harboured a deep resentment towards her for making them move out of the city—something that made her father nervous.

She stepped in off the balcony. He was still going on about moving to Canada, throwing things around, and blaming her for their desperate situation. She'd had enough. "Canada? Really? And never see my dad? Not going to happen, Phil. We actually need him. Don't you get that? All we have to do is get in touch."

"No!" he roared.

She wasn't having it. Fuck it, she'd listened to enough of his ranting. "If you want your precious city life back with your *mates*, all we have to do is get in touch with him. He'd have us moved in with him in a blink. And you know it." The venom in her tone surprised her, almost as much as gesturing inverted commas for *mates*. The baby wouldn't stop kicking, and Phil's voice had been grating at her all morning. Couldn't he see what he was doing to her?

Of course, she should have known better than to rise to him—it always ended in him flipping the lid. Her words had stung him, it was obvious in his silence, though his glare was louder than anything so far—a sure sign that he saw nothing now but the red mist descending over his mind. His words were gone, and she knew from experience that he only had one way to go.

He stormed towards her, closing the space between them—his eyes almost glowing with rage—and grabbed her by the throat, her breath bursting from her when he slammed her against the wall, lifting her tiny frame so she only had her tippy toes to stand on. She tried to call his name, but his vice-like grip prevented anything more than a panicked croak as his brown eyes glazed over, his teeth grinding in a snot-smeared snarl. Her lungs screamed for air, and the baby kicked everything within reach, so hard she couldn't stop herself pissing, the warmth a slight relief from the building pressure in her head.

"Don't ever say that again! You hear me?"

Though her vision was hazy from the lack of air, she noticed how his eyes narrowed and his pupils shrank back into two black beads.

"I'm the man of this house," he snapped, his spit bouncing off her face. "I'll fucking provide! I don't need help from your cunt of a father. The great fucking Joseph Greene."

And as quick as it had begun, it was over. He released his grip and backed off, and she dropped to her knees, coughing and hacking, touching the burning flesh he'd almost pushed through in his manic attack. She didn't miss the change in his eyes as she gasped for air, her lungs screaming to be filled.

The room spun, and bile rose in her throat. Phil knelt beside her and wrapped his arms around her. At first, she attempted to fight him off, but at the same time she wanted the loving embrace. It could have been anyone's, but it was his. And he was all she had these days now her relationship with her father had become cold and distant.

"I'm sorry, babe," he whispered into her ear. 'I'm so sorry."

She couldn't bring herself to look at him, but acknowledged his sentiment with a grunt, figuring that beneath all the rage he was just a frustrated man—a man under pressure—a lonely man. She remembered and tried to understand how hard it must have been for him to come all the way out here with her. Back in the city, he'd been a top chef for a respected restaurant, while now he was just a part-timer struggling to get the hours in the kitchen in the local pub. His passion was obvious, and he had so much of it for his work, but now that desire was all but dead, and he hated it, and it showed in his constant resentment. But she lived with the hope that, once the baby came, he'd start appreciating what he had instead of lusting after impossible aspirations. Most of his close friends had moved on with their lives and started to settle down, leaving Phil behind to hang around with some random acquaintances who only cared about drinking and fucking around.

"I didn't mean to hurt you," he continued, stroking her head, the French seeping into his accent again. "It's just the pressure of it all. The changes. The baby. Sometimes I can't take it and it gets to me." He shuddered as a loud sob escaped. "And the money. We've no fucking money."

His vulnerability pained her heart—she wasn't used to seeing him so weak. It was his brutish side that attracted her when they'd met five years ago, soon after her mother departed, when she'd worked in the restaurant with him. She'd always had a thing for hard men, and Phil had lived up to that, pursuing her aggressively until he won her over, but not without warning off all her male friends in the process. Even so, she didn't mind this too much if it meant she got to settle down and gain some stability in her life by starting a family with her Alpha male.

"It's okay," she said, patting his back. "It's okay. I know how hard it's been on you."

She hugged him then and they sat silent against the wall, staring through the open balcony doors. The sun had slithered behind clouds, and a cool breeze brought an unwanted chill into the apartment—maybe a sign of more wintery things to come.

The baby was active again, kicking away at her insides, so she nudged Phil aside to caress her bump. She couldn't help but smile at the impact of every elbow and kick against her hands.

"What's he doing?" Phil asked, his face expressionless, his eyes shadowed.

"It's little Monti saying hello. I think someone wants out." She rubbed her swollen abdomen.

"Monti?" His eyebrows raised. "As in, Montague? Not Greene, like you wanted?"

"Nah... We'll get through this rough patch, babe. We're a family. I just want us all to be happy. Anyway, who says it's a boy?" She smiled and looked away, then bit down on her nail, dragged her teeth underneath in an effort to get to the itch. It was always the case—no matter how much she dug, she could never get to it.

She caught his nod, taking it to be one of approval, and breathed a sigh of relief that his pride was somewhat restored. It hadn't been her choice to keep the Greene family name attached. Her dad, as expected, had applied so much pressure on her—subtle and direct. Legacy meant everything to Joseph Greene, and without ever having a son of his own, he'd pinned all his hopes on this grandson to continue his lineage.

Phil bent so his ear was against her bump. "Hmm, I think you're right about someone wanting to get out." He sat up and looked at her. "Let's bring him for a spin. We're cracking up in this place, stuck in day after day. Fancy going for a drive?"

When you suffer from cabin fever, sometimes the simplest ideas sound like the best ones. Erin perked up with a childish excitement. "Eh, yeah. Can we go somewhere to watch the sunset? Maybe View Point?" Her eyes brimmed with a watery eagerness. Being cooped up all day wasn't her style. She loved the outdoors. Getting out and about in the fresh air always eased her anxiety. She wasn't one for isolation, often fearing her thoughts, and the way they tended to plague her mind. Her father knew this and took her trekking up the Wicklow Mountains when she was younger as often as he could.

Lusk sat alone in the flat farmlands of Fingal County, and while it possessed a beauty of its own, hiking around here just wasn't the same. She loved what the mountains had to offer: forests, history, ruins and legends, and hoped to instil that same love in her child.

"Yeah, of course," Phil answered, jumping up, full now of a new sense of confidence. "Believe it or not, I was actually going to suggest that today. There's snow forecast for later, but we'll be back well before that hits. And I know you love it up there, so it's the perfect place to go on such a nice afternoon." He helped her to her feet, then pulled out his set of keys and gave them a jingle. "It's going on three o'clock now, and we've a bit of a drive. Let's get moving, yeah?"

The key to his old beat-up Ford Mondeo was on display for Erin to see. They hated the car, mostly because it was a big financial burden on them. "I'll be right there, just going to change out of these clothes really quick."

She slipped into their room to change into fresh underwear and a clean pair of maternity jeans. The smell of urine as she peeled away her soiled pants had her gagging, and when she looked at herself in the mirror, she couldn't help but shiver with the shame of soiling herself. She swallowed it back. He hadn't meant it. His red mist blinded him to everything—she'd seen it often enough, and how regretful he was after.

With slow deep breaths, she regained her composure. The last thing she needed was for Phil to become even more stressed out. He shouted in to her again, his voice growing more impatient with every call. With a final glance in the mirror, she turned and left the room, knowing it would be unwise to keep him waiting any longer.

"Will the car make it?" she asked, deflecting his attention.

"Course it will. Come on, it'll be grand."

She stopped as they headed for the door. "Do we need to take anything with us?"

"Nah, sure it's roasting out. Snow's not due 'til tonight. Here, grab my coat there and we'll get going." He pulled a black, woollen jumper over his head and slung a rucksack over his shoulder, its contents clinking from the swing.

Erin removed the coat from the hook by the door and tucked it under her arm with her handbag.

"That's grand. And don't be worrying, we'll be back well before the weather turns bad."

"I don't know, Phil. Are you sure?"

He followed her out into the hallway. "Sure, they're always getting their forecasts wrong in this bleedin' country. It's a smashing day, so let's not waste it hanging around this hole."

She laughed and shrugged at the same time, but a voice in the back of her head told her she wasn't as sure as he was. "How are we for petrol?"

"Plenty. I only filled it up the other day."

"Are you sure? You know how much of a guzzler that yoke is."

"Ah, will you stop moaning and groaning. We're having some family time, out in the fresh air. Let's enjoy it. It's no wonder my head is the way it is being stuck in this kip so much."

He wrapped his arm around her and guided her down the stairs as they headed for the car. Outside, the twin round towers of St Macuillin's Church dominated the horizon at the end of the street.

"Hey," Erin said, "did you know that Cuchulain's wife, Emer, was born in Lusk?"

"Yeah? I've a vague memory of being told in school that she was really jealous and wanted to kill anyone sniffing around her fella, or something like that."

"So legend has it. If this baby is a girl, maybe

we can call her Emer. Wouldn't that be cool?"

He frowned, but only for a split-second. "I suppose. Not sure if I want to be associated with this village any more than I have to be. Anyway, didn't they drink a potion to make them forget about some sort of affair?"

"Erm...not sure."

He opened the car door for her and she ducked her head and got in.

"Might be nice to have something like that so we could forget our fights."

She nodded in silent agreement, then pulled her hand away when she realised she was touching her throat.

TWO

It was hardly a holiday, but aside from the obvious tension, it was still better than being cooped up indoors surrounded by bad vibes. The gammy old radio struggled to get a clear reception, but still managed to blast out Fleetwood Mac's *Go Your Own Way* as Phil drove along the M50 motorway towards the mountains to the south of the city. With it being a Sunday afternoon, the roads were relatively clear and the drive was pleasant enough, with the two of them sitting silent, listening to the music.

Erin couldn't help but think Buckingham's lyrics were aimed at their relationship. She threw Phil a glace and wondered if he was thinking about going his own way, maybe after

Geoff Baron. She hoped not. Geoff was a bad influence and she was glad to see the back of him. They'd never got on, anyway. It was as if he held it against her for taking his best friend away from him.

After driving around the hills for a couple of hours, stopping here and there to take in the beautiful scenery, they arrived at View Point— the sun struggling against a bank of dark clouds creeping across the horizon. To Erin, it looked more like rain was coming, not snow, though you'd never know in Ireland, with four seasons in one day being nothing out of the ordinary.

View Point was a small, forest car park that overlooked the city from near the top of the hills. Two other cars occupied spaces near them, but far enough away not to be overlooked. In the surrounding woodland, most of the broadleaf trees were turning, but still full of life and colour, and in the valley below, the first signs of winter were nowhere to be seen.

As they sat there, taking in the panoramic splendour before them, a pale white moon hung low in the east, beginning its journey into the night. Erin loved the gentle glow it provided as a counter to the setting sun—a beacon of security, like a nightlight in a child's room. She rubbed her bump at the thought of her baby sleeping without any worries under such a light.

The strong forest scent filled the car as they watched nature's evening show. She touched the back of Phil's hand, filling her lungs with mountain air, and in that moment, in spite of everything, they were at peace.

She glanced at the clock on the dashboard. Six-thirty. It was still about an hour before darkness would blanket the mountains. They'd missed dinner and, without noticing, were the only ones left in the car park.

She groaned. "I'm hungry."

Phil reached in behind her seat and rustled about in his rucksack. "I figured we wouldn't be back in time. Here, have some of this." He handed her a homemade smoothie. "I made it earlier for you. It's your favourite."

Apple and banana flavour in a keep-cup—a staple in her diet over the last eight months. She thought about the fight earlier, if something as one-sided could be called a fight. It was so intense, but a million miles from the peace and serenity they were sharing now—a young couple experiencing a romantic moment on a mountain—almost worth going through to be able to enjoy it. Anyway, they were just going through a phase—a tough time. He loved her, and she loved him. Most couples their age were the same, right? Their struggles weren't unique to them. Things would get better and they would become a complete family soon enough.

She was sure their bundle of joy would bring them closer.

She sipped on her smoothie and savoured the ever-changing visual before them. "This is fantastic." She smiled at him. "Can I ask you a question, babe?"

"Sure."

"What do you really want in life?"

He didn't answer straight away, taking time to ponder, as she expected. Then he looked away and sighed, "To be happy and free, I suppose."

Her stomach rumbled. "Time for food. Let's head home, babe. It's been a long day."

The last of the sun's rays penetrated the windscreen with an intense orange hue that lit up Phil's face. He didn't reply, raising his hand instead to shield his eyes as he stared at her. She sensed unease in him, and his shoulders jerked as he released another, deeper, sigh. So much for coming here to relax. He was on the edge. She knew it, seeing from his almost glazed-over eyes that his mind was racing with a million different thoughts. But she didn't want to say something that might set him off again. His unhappiness couldn't be masked, and he was too easily triggered when in such a state.

Instead, she attacked her nail again, this time succeeding in tearing the offending sliver off. A trickle of blood seeped from the exposed flesh. She winced and tucked her hand in under her arm, relishing the deep throb.

Phil turned the key in the ignition while he stared off into the distance. It took three attempts before the Mondeo spluttered and coughed into life. Music filled the interior again and the handbrake creaked as he released it. He reversed out of their spot, then shifted forward, the tyres scraping over compacted gravel, with chippings pinging off the underbody of the beat-up car.

As they turned onto the hill, he removed his foot from the brake and gravity took hold of the vehicle on its journey down into the valley. Erin closed her eyes. The smoothie had settled her stomach, allowing the car's gentle motion ease her into a quiet place.

THREE

She awoke from her slumber when the car shunted. They were in the basin of a valley, and Phil had obviously engaged the gears now that the road had levelled off. She rubbed her tired eyes and sat up. On either side, steep hills full of tall pine trees rose into the evening sky, blocking any remaining light from the ebbing sun. She rubbed her upper arms and shoulders, and noticed the tarmac ahead glistening, signalling the expected fall in temperature as the evening crept into night.

"Where are we? How long was I out?"

"A while, so I decided to take the scenic route. But its fine, we'll stop for a coffee at the next garage."

As he drove along the valley road, it was hard

to ignore his struggle to keep the car beyond a certain speed. Erin admired his determination to keep it moving along, constantly shifting gears and coaxing it with swear words and a few frustrated growls. She also noticed that he was losing the battle.

Then it ground to a halt.

"What is it? What's wrong?"

"I don't know, babe. I'm giving it everything here, but we aren't moving." He slapped the steering wheel and groaned deep in his throat, a sound she'd learned to take heed off.

Time after time, he turned the key, but all he got was a screeching and stuttering response from the motor. Then the engine kicked into life, as it always did, and he whooped with joy, shifted into first, moved forward for a few metres, until the car shuddered and groaned and, within a few seconds, died with an audible whimper.

"Phil, what the hell is happening?" Her voice was edged with tension as a rumbling panic crept through her.

"I don't know. Don't be alarmed, but I think we may be out of juice." He shrugged, a gesture she knew well—one that said it wasn't his fault.

"What? Are you serious?" she screamed. "I'm eight months pregnant here. I..." She looked around as a blanket of shadow spread through the woodland on both sides. Night was falling fast. "We need to get home."

"Okay, relax. Just chill out for a second. I could be wrong. I'm sure I put enough in it, so it might be something simple."

"In the engine?"

"Probably."

"Well, go check it out, will you? It's nearly pitch-black." She rubbed her shoulders again.

"Don't be so dramatic. I'm sure it's nothing major." He got out and grabbed his coat. "I'll, eh...take a look." He went around and opened up the bonnet.

While she waited, she looked back along the road. Everything around lay silent, with not even a bird singing now the light was gone from this part of the forest.

The silence was broken by a series of clicks, probably Phil tinkering with the engine. She hadn't a clue about such things. But then a light flashed under the hood and she realised it was his cigarette lighter. God, she'd love a smoke now, but it wasn't going to happen—she'd given them up as soon as she fell pregnant. Still...

Phil walked around the car, his coat on, blowing a plume of smoke out. Erin shuddered. There was a definite chill in the air. And it was so quiet. She rubbed her bump. Baby was asleep, which was one good thing, though her earlier unease hadn't dissipated.

With the engine off, she couldn't buzz the window down, so she opened the door, the frigid air catching her breath. "Well? Any luck?"

He gave her a thumbs-up, then took a last drag from his fag before stamping it out, the sparks fluttering like fireflies in the gloom.

She slammed the door shut and let out a long-drawn sigh. Her stomach gurgled again, and she pushed visions of a hot Sunday dinner out of her head.

Phil climbed back in and tried the ignition again, but the engine didn't even jolt this time, and she knew it had given up the fight. The fumes in the engine weren't sufficient to spark it into life.

"Did you check the gauge before we left?" she asked.

"Yeah, of course I did."

"How much was in it then?"

"I don't know. Half a tank, or thereabouts."

"Jesus, Phil, I can't believe we're stuck out here in the middle of fucking nowhere." She puffed out another frustrated sigh and dug her fingers into her scalp, kneading away at the building tension. "I mean, you're the one who suggested coming all the way up here, and then didn't even check the gauge? We're miles from the nearest station."

"Shut up," he barked. "I said I checked it." She stared at him and he put his hands up in apology. "I'm sorry, babe. I was just so happy to get out of the apartment, it slipped my mind, or

I thought I'd checked it." He produced another one of his shrugs. "I'm not sure."

They sat in a heavy silence for a while. Erin shook her head and just stared out the passenger window, the hunger kicking in and her tummy groaning in protest rather than just gurgling.

"Okay, I think I know what happened."

She rolled her eyes but didn't say anything. There was no point when Phil had an idea in his head.

"Babe?"

"Well, go on then," she snapped.

"I think the gauge is broken."

She turned and looked at him. "Broken?"

"Yeah. Watch. Check this out." He turned the key in the ignition. The engine didn't engage, but the meters on the dashboard lit up—the oil bar raising, followed by the temperature indicator, but the fuel gauge didn't move. Nothing.

He repeated the process twice more, looking at her and nodding each time. "See, I couldn't have known. It wasn't my fault."

She closed her eyes and groaned. What was the point? They were out of petrol and there was nothing to be done about it. The night was upon them, and here they were, somewhere deep in the Wicklow Mountains, stranded.

PART TWO

FOUR

With the sun set and darkness upon them, most families around the country were probably preparing to sit down to their evening tea. But this wasn't on the cards for Erin and Philip as they sat in their car, marooned deep in the Wicklow Mountains.

"Well, genius," she snapped, "how are we going to get out of this one?"

Phil snorted as he shrugged. "Well, babe, to be honest, there's not a whole lot we can do with a car with no petrol."

She glared at him, fighting back the urge to just scream out all her fears and frustrations. How in the hell could he be taking this so lightly? She gnawed on another nail.

"I supposed we'll have to walk to the nearest village."

She closed her eyes and bit harder.

"Don't worry, babe. If I remember right, it's only about forty minutes away."

She stared at him again, then sighed and shook her head.

"What?" he asked, his shoulders up around his ears. "We can be there before the garage shuts, get petrol, come back, and be home by midnight at the latest."

"I'm eight-months pregnant, Philip. I barely walk to the toilet at home, let alone forty fucking minutes up the road. Which is now covered in ice, by the way. Or haven't you bothered to look?" Tears ran down her cheeks and she cradled her head in her hands.

"There's always something with us," she said. "Isn't there? We can never just have a nice evening without something happening to ruin it." She looked at him, her vision blurred. "Do you even know where we are?"

He just stared back at her, his mouth open. "Eh…of course I do. I drove south over the hills towards Glendalough. We're not too far from the motorway."

Glendalough. Christ. She couldn't bring herself to get involved in another argument with him. Her energy was sapped and her limbs felt so lethargic she could hardly raise her arms.

"Okay, look, babe, I'll go on. I'll jog on up in that direction." He gestured up the road with his thumb. "I'm pretty sure I know where the garage is and I'll be back here within an hour. Tops."

She let out a long sigh. "Let's just ring my dad. He'll come get us."

Like a red rag to a bull, Phil went from zero to vex in less than a microsecond. "For fuck's sake, Erin, why does everything have to go back to your father? We ran out of petrol. Big deal. Shit happens. Just stay here and relax. I'll sort this out. Haven't I always taken care of you?"

She leaned back, too aware of that look. His temper was close to going through the roof.

"I'm sick of good ol' Joseph being your solution to every little hiccup we have. Joseph fucking Green, who, by the way, hasn't even spoken to you since you moved out." He huffed, looked around him, then punched the steering wheel.

"Hey!" she screamed, unable to hold it back. "Go on then. Go get the fucking petrol. Hard man Monti punching steering wheels. Grow up, will you? Go on, get away from us."

The ensuing silence was deafening. He stared at her through surprised eyes, then shrugged and got out, slamming the door after him. She watched him walk to the front of the car, where he stopped and took a deep breath. He stroked his beard, a habit of his when working things through, and then walked around to the passenger window, where he tapped on the glass with a pale-white knuckle.

"Babe?"

She blinked tears out of weary eyes but said nothing.

"I've left the keys with you." His voice was muffled through the glass. "Lock yourself in, okay? I promise I won't be long."

She didn't reply, and he shrugged again and moved away from the car, shaking his head. As his figure blurred with the gloom, she opened the door and pulled herself out. "Try and bring back something nice to eat. Please?"

He turned and laughed, then ran back and took her into a gentle hug, his beard ruffling off her tender neck. Even in a shit situation, he still managed to amuse her. It was why she loved him, and ultimately why she couldn't live without him. Despite his awful tempers, he had a quirky manner about him that never failed to endear him to her. She was well aware that he resented how aspects of their lives had turned out, and hated her father being in the mix, but she loved him so much that his jealousy and category-five flare-ups could almost always be shrugged off.

"I'll do my best. Look, I promise I won't be long. I know where I'm going. I'll be back before you know it. I love you."

"I love you, too."

He gave her another hug, then bent and kissed her bump. "Bye, bye, little buddy." Then he kissed her cheek and guided her back into the car. "Stay inside, right?"

She just nodded and watched again as he faded into the gloom. When he disappeared, she pushed the buttons on each door down, the act sealing her in and bringing on an uneasy sense of isolation. She didn't like being alone, and as she sat there, looking at the darkness where Phil had been a moment ago, the silence hit her with an impact she hadn't expected—all force, no sound.

Her anxiety deepened, and the throbbing from her bloodied finger didn't help. Being alone was something she'd never got used to, but here she sat in solitude, lost in the Wicklow Mountains, afraid of the thoughts and emotions swirling through her.

FIVE

Erin always wanted to be the master of her own emotions, but could never fully manage to take hold of her life. For reasons she didn't really understand, she allowed pain and violence in—almost embracing it—her desperate love for Phil often the only bulwark against complete annihilation; his penchant for violence echoing deep in her soul.

Dark clouds blocked out the glow of the full moon, engulfing the road in darkness. Then the snow arrived. At first it fell soft and gentle, but it didn't take long before it came down in relentless flurries, blanketing the old Ford. The road quickly disappeared, and even though Erin used the wipers, her visibility decreased with every hard-fought swipe—the rubber sticking and ribbing as it struggled against the snowy build-up, causing the wiper motor to seize every few seconds—the overworked electronic device whining in protest.

She fought for breath as panic gripped her. What seemed like ages ago now, they'd sat watching the sun go down, and now, here she was, alone, hoping Phil would appear at the top of the road with a small tank of petrol under his arm. But he hadn't returned, his absence compounding her concern about the worsening weather conditions. She gnawed at her nail. Where was he? If he got caught in the blizzard, he could freeze to death. The terror of that possibility had her heart skipping, and she fought to catch her breath, each fitful exhalation a plume of vapour, further fogging up the car windows.

Her fearful focus was broken by a vibration coming from her handbag on the floor. Her phone. She lunged for her bag and pulled it out. The eight o'clock daily reminder to take her birth-control pill. Before she was pregnant, of course. Out of sheer laziness, she'd never bothered to cancel it. Groaning, she stabbed at the screen with her forefinger. Then it dawned on her that she was holding a phone. It had been in her bag all day and she'd never once thought of it. Her heart lifted at the prospect of contacting Phil to see how far away he was. The beat-up phone had seen better days, surviving being dropped twice from a height and once submerged in a toilet. Despite this, it still functioned, now actually receiving a faint signal, even with her being in the pit of a dark valley.

Without hesitation, she tapped into the address book and selected Phil's number. It didn't surprise her when it took a while to connect, especially with the hills being so steep on either side. When it did, an automated woman's voice answered: *"The customer you are calling is unavailable at this time. Please try again later."*

She tried a couple more times, but the annoying answering machine kept telling her what she didn't want to hear. Groaning—almost growling—she slapped the glovebox. The worry flooded back, apprehension gripping her as she feared the worst for Phil. If something happened to him, how would anyone know where she was? How long would it take people to realise she was missing? She'd started her maternity leave two days ago, finally bowing to Phil's constant pressure to stay at home. It was bad enough getting from Lusk to the hospital as it stood, the last thing they wanted was to go into labour while in the office. She was self-conscious enough as it was and didn't want her colleagues seeing her waters burst all over her chair. Needless to say, the good people at Elliot and

Sons Accountancy where not expecting a call from her anytime soon. Back in Lusk, they were yet to make any real friends, or even properly introduce themselves to their neighbours, and the rent wasn't due for another three weeks, so their landlord wouldn't notice a thing.

The snow grew heavier, the wind swirling it into small drifts against the windscreen. She tried phoning a few of her friends, but all efforts failed to connect any further than an answering machine.

As each long minute passed, she fought a sense of growing desperation, and even though she figured it was her own mind working against her, that knowledge made the situation seem worse than it actually was. If she were to call the emergency services now and then moments later Phil turned up, it would be the height of embarrassment. Still, she couldn't get a grip on the stress spiralling through her. Panic raced up her back with a surprisingly warm sensation that flushed through her body. With only one bar left on her battery, she decided it was time for the last resort. She scrolled down to the number and pressed call. It only took a moment to connect, and she took a shaky breath when it started to ring.

"Hello, Erin? Is that you?" The tone was stern and she didn't know how to respond—it had been so long since she'd heard his voice.

"Hello!" he barked into her ear.

She took another deep breath, her hand on her swollen abdomen.

"Hi, Daddy."

The ensuing silence had her squirming in her seat. The pair hadn't spoken since herself and Phil moved to Lusk against his wishes.

Joseph Greene was a ruthless, yet successful businessman. For the last five years, his company had returned substantial profit annually, his empire expanding primarily because of his cut-throat ambition. It got to a point where Erin couldn't walk around the city without his presence following her. This affected Philip more than anyone. He couldn't bear her father's attitude towards him, as he felt his profession was always an issue, viewed as inferior and insufficient.

She loved Phil so much that it didn't matter what his job was. He could be an astronaut or a binman for all she cared—it didn't matter. He was a chef. A good chef. He was her chef and her whole world, and this drove her father berserk.

"How... How are you, Princess?" her father stammered down the phone. The shock of the out-of-the-blue phone call had clearly caught him off-guard. She remembered the last time they'd spoken, the night before she'd moved out, forced to pick between him and her fiancé.

"Daddy, I...need your help," she said, cutting straight to the point. She blurted out the details, telling him about how they'd gone on a Sunday drive into the mountains, and how she was now stranded on the side of the road, somewhere unknown to her.

"Where's whatisname?' Joseph asked. 'Phil, isn't it?"

She closed her eyes, not surprised at her father's game-playing. The old man always got a jab in whenever Phil came up in conversation. She couldn't understand why he saw the love of her life as some sort of rival. Whatever his reason, that's the way he was—there was nothing to be done about it now. She sat upright. "He went to get help, Daddy, and he hasn't come back yet. I think something's happened to him." Tears welled and she couldn't hold back the sobs queuing in her throat.

The baby reacted by kicking into her ribs, something that had increased over the last hour or so.

"Calm down, Princess, calm down. Look, say no more, I get it. But I need to know where you are or else I can't help you." His firm boardroom voice softened. "The storm is only getting started."

She wiped the window and looked into a dark wall of falling snow, the persistent flurries consuming visibility. "We stopped in one of the valleys."

"You need to be more specific, love."

"It's dark, Daddy. There are woods on either side of the road. I can't tell for sure, but I know we're in the Wicklow Mountains somewhere?"

"Jesus, Erin, that could be anywhere. Can you take a look around, or get out to see if there are signposts—some sort of landmark that can help me zone in on your whereabouts?"

"What? I can't get out in this, Daddy. It's a blizzard out there!"

"Look, you don't have to go far. Just take a quick look around and see if there's anything that you can point me to."

She turned the headlights on full and got out, the glare reflecting back off the windblown flurries in almost a solid wall of white. Wiping her eyes, all she could make out was snow, trees, more snow, and more trees. A rush of blood and nerves shot up the back of her legs and her heart fluttered, her anxiety washing over her like a dark wave. "Daddy... I can't..." But then she noticed a small brown signpost up on the side of the road. Though barely visible, it was there, and it could lead to salvation. She placed the phone back inside the car, clutched her bump and made her way over to the sign, crunching the loosely packed snow at every step. With the near-blizzard conditions, she had to go right up to the sign to read it.

Lugnaquilla Mountain Park.

She couldn't hold back her smile. Finally, a lucky break, and something to work with. With a scream of delight, she almost ran back across the road, the headlights throwing her exaggerated silhouette onto the falling wall of snow. She got into the car, picked up the phone, and with an excited burst of breath, shouted what she'd read. Her voice crackled from the cold and she wiped dripping snot from her nose. "Daddy, you there?"

A long silence ensued, and she had to check to make sure she was still connected. "Daddy? Hello?"

"Erin, love, did you say Lugnaquilla? The Mountain Park, or just the actual mountain?"

"The Park. Does that help, or what?"

"Are you one-hundred-percent certain?"

"Yes, Daddy, I'm certain. Why?"

"Okay, listen to me carefully. Wrap up warm. It's going to take me some time to get up there. With this weather, the roads are going to be treacherous."

She didn't like that response. "But...how long will you be?"

"Listen, Erin. It's going to take me a while, but that isn't the only issue here."

She listened hard as her father disclosed his main concerns, telling her that the extended area was heavily populated with deer, which needed to be culled every year. And this year, because hunting had been banned to combat the scourge of unlicensed hunters using unregistered firearms, the authorities had come up with a green solution to the problem. The squared area from Donard to Glendalough, and Glenmalure to Rathdongan had been fenced in, and grey wolves were introduced into the enclosed area to see if the deer population could be kept in check in a more natural way. When she asked how he knew all this, it turned out that the Irish Wolf Conservation Trust was in the middle of this zone, and he was the trust's main financial backer, chairman of the board, and brainchild behind the project.

"Wolves, Daddy, are you serious?" She shuddered from a combination of cold and fear. The interior of the car spun, and she held onto the dash to steady herself. All she needed now was to start getting sick from the thoughts flooding back into her mind at the very mention of the beasts. She remembered how the wind sounded like howling on the day of her mother's funeral. Hailstones clattered against the closed coffin as she stood in disbelief. Her father was distant that day, the pain in his eyes on show for all to see. She chalked it up as shock and wasn't surprised when he smothered her with love—he'd always been over-protective— and she'd given him a pass, but also began to distance herself from the overbearingness of it all. Perhaps leaving him alone was the wrong thing—never in a million years did she expect him to obsess over the animal that decimated their family.

"Yes, love. I acquired the land a while ago and launched the trust a little over a month ago. From now on, until I get there, please stay inside the car. Remain calm and wait for me. I'll find you."

"But, wolves? Who the fuck made the decision to put wolves up here? What about hikers?"

"I did, Princess. People aren't supposed to be walking around an area that's closed off to the public. It was advertised quite a bit over the last few months. How could Phil be so stupid? He should've known if he was driving around those hills."

"Oh, God. Please hurry, Daddy. The baby. We're hungry and scared."

"I know, Princess, I'm on the way. Just do me a favour, will you?"

"Of course, what is it?"

"Just stay inside the car. You'll be safe in there. And most importantly, can you please—"

"Daddy? Hello." She looked at the phone. "No. No!" But it was dead. She roared at it and slapped and punched the dash and passenger door. The interior spun again and shivers rushed through her, and even when she tried to slow her breathing, counting through her exhalations to get it together, her mind wouldn't follow—all kinds of worst-case scenarios racing through her head.

Surely Phil wouldn't have been stupid enough to drive into an area filled with wolves? How did he get the car in, and what if they got him on his way to the garage? On his way back? Hyperventilating, she held her bump and resorted to prayer, calling to an unknown force from above for Phil to return safely.

SIX

In her darkest moments, she would come home to her parents' house to find him waiting outside for her in their crappy Mondeo. To cast out the shadows that consumed her, they would use the ultimate weapon—chat. For hours they would lie together on the bed in her attic room. Her walls were decorated with occult posters and rock stars, with one in particular—her absolute favourite, and the centrepiece of her collage—an early pic of Quartorn from Bathory. Phil didn't get jealous back then, or if he did, he hid it well. Needless to say, he thought her interests and taste in music strange and hard to take. She came to the conclusion that it must be hard to be jealous of something you don't understand. But this didn't stop them becoming inseparable, forming a bond that would challenge all around them, and it started with talking, sometimes for hours, learning everything about each other, including their flaws. They would tuck away on the third floor, smoke, drink, fuck, and enjoy each other with the skylight window open. The crisp spring air filtered in and engulfed the room in a beautiful fresh scent. Indeed, the weather was great when they first met.

Now, the blizzard raged around her, the Mondeo consumed in snow. Inside, she was doing her best to keep it together, focusing on happy memories, but her mind seemed to be working overtime against her, swelled her anxiety levels beyond healthy. The interior of the car would have been pitch-black if it wasn't for the low-wattage blub on the ceiling illuminating what could only be described as the inside of a fridge. An abiding undercurrent of panic gripped her, threatening to choke all sense of reality, yet somewhere within all the despair, she clung to Phil—to hope.

Phil was no fool. He'd be sheltered somewhere safe for the night. No way would he make it back to the car, and even if he did, they wouldn't be going anywhere without a few hours of hard labour digging out the snow, not to mention the road out of the valley that could probably only be cleared by a plough.

As she finally accepted the inevitability of her situation, she settled into having to stay the night, alone, waiting for the storm to pass. Then in the morning, Phil would come to her aid. Or Dad. That brought a chuckle, imagining the two of them turning up together from different directions.

She shivered, clutched her bump, and sang softly to it, then apologised out loud for allowing herself to get into this mess. At first, she blamed Phil for making such a stupid decision to take them into the valley, but she didn't have the energy to maintain her anger. Her tummy groaned again, famished, and her baby knew it. Apart from the panic of her situation, all her thoughts focused on her hunger. Why hadn't they brought food with them? Now, looking at the empty smoothie bottle, she couldn't remember a time when they hadn't taken snacks or sandwiches with them on their long drives.

To stop thinking of food, she took herself back a few months to when she decided to leave home to live in Lusk with Phil. Financially, it made sense—they couldn't afford anywhere in or around the city—and Phil wanted them to live together, to see the baby in. But in reality, their relationship was already seriously strained when they received the keys from the letting agent. Phil's pride and jealousy was always a stumbling block in their decisions, with him refusing every bit of help offered out of a stubborn sense of obligation, and in doing so hindering many of their plans. It came as no surprise considering he shared near-identical traits with her father.

She blinked away tears, her teeth chattering as shivers raced through her. Why hadn't she brought her coat? So stupid. Phil couldn't be blamed for taking his with him. How else was he to stay warm on his way to the garage? She looked around for something to wrap herself in. Daddy did tell her to wrap up warm, after all. Perhaps he knew all along she'd be here for the night?

All she saw on the back seat were empty sweet wrappers and plastic Coke bottles that only had a flat dribble left in them. She sighed and hugged herself. Loneliness was casting a darker shadow now, and boredom. One reason she hated being alone was her low-attention span. She'd always been that way, and her father hadn't let her forget it. Phil understood— he'd got her a new smartphone to keep her occupied. She loved it, and the many ways it connected her to the outside world. If only she'd remembered to charge it. She turned it on again, surprised to see it spark to life, but only with two-percent battery power. And when she phoned Phil again, that woman's obnoxious pre-recorded voice began to speak, only to be cut off when the phone died for a second time.

"Fuck." It came out as more of a growl as she flung the phone onto the floor. There had to be something in the bloody car. She looked in the glovebox, but it contained nothing of use— nothing to keep her warm, anyway.

She rummaged in her bag again. At the bottom, she found a blister pack with two pills still encased. Her Xanax. She couldn't believe she'd forgotten about them. Her doctor had cancelled her prescription earlier in the year due to misuse, but that didn't stop her sourcing them from the internet. He'd warned her to only use them in extreme circumstances—she figured this qualified. With a quick pop and without a second thought, she dropped one into her mouth, gulping as the chalk coating stuck to the inside of her throat. Then another one—a double dose she hoped would make the shadows retreat and knock her out for the night.

As she lay back in the seat, she remembered the boot of the car. She sat up. How in the hell hadn't she thought of it, or what it might hold?

With a new sense of mission, she whipped the keys from the ignition and stuffed them into her jeans' pocket. Opening the door caught her up short with the weight of the snow against it. It wasn't happening, basically because she wasn't strong enough. She had no choice but to let the back of her seat down, climb in behind, and lay across the seat. Using her feet, she pushed against the door to force it open. A gust of ice-cold wind burst in, peppering her face with freezing snow. With a yelp, she shook it off and pushed harder. It worked—the space was just about wide enough for herself and her baby bump to exit. She struggled across the seats to get outside.

The blizzard was ferocious, and it only took a few seconds for the chill to eat into her. All she wanted to do was jump back into the relative security of the car, but she had to see if there was anything of value in the boot.

She shut the door and pushed forward, keeping against the car as each footstep sank into the drifting snow. "Christ, Philip, what the hell have you got me into?"

The wind battered her, and she had to kick and push snow out of the way to get around to the boot. She used touch to locate the lock, which she prayed wouldn't be frozen shut. That wouldn't have surprised her considering how cold she felt after just a minute out of the car. She sighed with relief when the key fitted in without a problem.

The boot cracked open and an awful smell hit her, but she held her breath and continued on. The storage space inside was lit by a small bulb. Snowflakes danced around as her eyes adjusted, and it only took a moment before she spotted an old pair of Phil's work boots beside his gym bag. She reached in and grabbed the boots, the stench catching her senses, a smell she'd become familiar with—from Phil's work kitchen. A quick look around located the cause: half-eaten rolls and bits of rotten meat where strewn about the space, even stuck in the grooves.

"For fuck's sakes, Phil." Her teeth chattered and her stomach turned, but she fought back her desire to puke. No time. It was so cold. The boots stank nearly as bad as the rank food. She used to order Phil to take them off before he came into the house, until he got so pissed off he started leaving them in the boot.

She coughed out another wave of nausea, leaned in, and grabbed the gym bag. When she ripped open its zipper, the same smell came rushing out, and this time she couldn't keep back the compulsion, heaving a small splash of vomit into the snow, the heat of it creating a hole down to the ground.

"Oh, God. What the fuck am I doing?"

She wiped her mouth and returned to the bag, first finding an unwashed chef's uniform—hat and apron included. They would help. She leaned out, took a deep breath, then pulled the clothing out of the way to find a set of professional-grade culinary knives in a white plastic sheath—complete with a plastic belt. Can't eat knives. She set them aside and checked out the uniform.

The white jacket and pants stank of Phil's sweat and were in dire need of a wash. At what point was he actually planning on cleaning them? For a man who took pride in his appearance, his lack of basic hygiene in this case surprised her. She knew about his boots, but this, it was like a Phil she didn't know.

However, at this point, there was no time to waste on such thoughts—these were extra layers, and even though they stank, they'd have to do. She stuffed the garments under her arm and was about to slam the boot shut when she noticed a lock, broken chain, and bolt cutters at the right side. Unusual things to have in a boot, but her fingers were going numb and she didn't have the energy or will to poke around further. She closed the boot, grabbed up Phil's footwear, and battled through the driven snow to the passenger door and the frigid safety of the car.

The cold back seat sent shivers up her spine as she struggled to put Phil's work trousers on over her jeans. The jacket was easy to manage and buttoned up tight over her hooded top. She then wrapped herself in the filthy apron—anything to help her keep warm. And it was better than nothing, but she was still freezing, so she climbed back into the front and put the key in the ignition to turn the heating on. Nothing happened—not even a light on the dash.

"Fuck!"

No petrol. A flat battery. Buried in a snowstorm. What more could go wrong?

The car shook from the gusts crashing against the side of it. The blizzard showed no sign of letting up—if anything, it was intensifying. Every now and then, she caught the sound of trees creaking in protest at the deluge. If it wasn't for the seriousness of her situation, it was almost a pleasure to hear nature put on a show of this magnitude. She raised the passenger seat up a little and tried to make herself comfortable.

As she lay staring at the ceiling, she tried her hardest to focus on something in the dark, but as her eyes strained, her mind cast back to the event surrounding her mother's tragic death. Five years ago, skiing in the French Alps, but it wasn't the slopes that got her. It was going off-track and falling victim to a wolf. Doctors and local news reported the beast to be unusually large—judging by the scale of her injuries. She fought hard for weeks—Joseph by her side every step of the way—but, ultimately, Helen Greene died. Erin recalled the change in her father—almost overnight. He grew resentful and angry with the world and drove all his energies into his business, and his protective nature over her strengthened until it became suffocating.

The tablets were kicking in. When she closed her eyes, scenarios and images flashed through her mind as the blizzard raged outside. She blinked them away and looked around, the pilot light flickering under the last gasps of the battery, allowing unwanted shadows to return.

She was trapped, and it was without doubt the loneliest night of her life.

SEVEN

Erin woke to an eerie silence she couldn't get a handle on. Why was it so quiet? She listened out for Phil's pottering about in the kitchen and looked forward to her morning coffee to break the spell before breakfast.

A chill bit into her and she opened her eyes to a dull darkness. Then it came to her: fuck, no Phil, no coffee, no broken spell. Her ears popped as she moved her jaw from left to right, working the stiffness out. She sat up, unable to tell what time of day it was, or how long she'd slept for. No matter, the extra pill had worked, allowing her to ignore the cold while she slept.

She turned the key in the ignition, just to see, but the radio remained quiet, and the heating didn't engage. The air was dank and stuffy, and Phil's filthy uniform didn't help. Without wasting time, she crawled into the rear, let her seat back up, and assumed the same position as before, pushing against the door with both feet. It took double the effort this time, her thighs burning, and when the door cracked open, freezing air raced in. At least it was fresh—so much better than the stench of Phil's work clothes. She pushed the door out further—the exertion worth it as daylight infused the interior with a warm amber glow. The beautiful sound of a songbird off somewhere in the trees lifted her heart. Its tune gave her hope, and the possibility of rescue.

The storm had passed. She stood on the doorframe, filled her lungs with fresh air, and took in her surroundings. The area had been left looking like a winter wonderland, the type you'd see on a postcard or in National Geographic. Around the car, the drifted snow was easily three or four-feet deep, making it look almost like an igloo.

She needed to piss so bad, so she shut the door and struggled and stumbled through the snow until she made it to the closest bank of trees, where she peeled down her layers and went for what felt like the longest wee she'd ever taken. In her drugged slumber, she'd been aware of the baby pushing hard on her bladder during the night. A heavy steam rose up, with a strong smell of urine. She didn't care, a new day had arrived, and she even found a little humour in the situation—her inner child making the most of it. The relief was sublime. Phil would be disgusted. Such a prude at times.

Smiling, she pulled up her pants and the two sets of trousers and made her way back to the car. She removed the apron and used it to clear the snow off the windows, popping some into her mouth to relieve her thirst. It was freezing, but melted fast, and she did it again, surprised how little water come from a handful of snow. She worked her way around the car. It wasn't easy, but clearing the windows felt important, and positive, and it would be good to have a clear view from inside.

All she could see was white in every direction. The snow that coated the road lay untouched. No footprints or tyre marks. She shook her head. Phil hadn't made it back, and this concerned her. He'd said the nearest town was less than an hour away, probably on the other side of the valley, so he had to be close. Her dad, however, could be a full day away, especially if it had snowed like this across Dublin.

She got back into the car and tried her phone again, but it remained dead, like the car battery. What was she to do? She couldn't spend another night here, with no food. Not a chance. She massaged her bump for a good few minutes, even managing to sing a couple of songs, all the while keeping an eye out for movement around her—signs of Phil or her dad, or anyone else coming to rescue her. But no-one came, and after what might have been an hour, she decided she couldn't wait any longer. The only way out of this valley was by foot. Her feet.

If she let it, her renewed sense of hope could easily dissipate, and she knew the only way to prevent that was to fill her heart with fire—a fire that would fuel her to take hold of life and allow her to rise up out of her dilemma.

As she retrieved the work boots from the back seat, memories of her mother came flooding back:

Always wrap up well before going out.

Her poor mother, savaged by a beast of a wolf. Who would have thought it could happen in this day and age? And then her father had to freak her out with that news about wolves being in some sanctuary in the national park. Not here, obviously. Phil would never have entered such a place. He'd have to be mad, anyway, to set off on foot with them in the vicinity.

She shook such thoughts from her head, took off her wet runners, and tried the boots on. To her surprise, they weren't as big and awkward as she'd expected, and she felt sure they'd be a big assist in getting through the snow. She got out and shook out the damp apron, folded it up, then stuffed it under her arm. The oversized chef jacket was buttoned up tight to her neck, as cosy as she could make it. Readying herself, she stared up the middle of the road in the direction Phil had left.

The baby kicked, and she took a few deep breaths, rubbing her bump until it calmed. She refused to let hunger trouble her any further this morning. Fate had given her, Erin Greene, a mission—she had somewhere to go and needed to focus on the task in hand. She popped more snow into her mouth, prepared herself mentally for the long struggle ahead and, with a deep breath, took her first step onto the freezing, snow-covered road, heading for salvation.

EIGHT

It didn't take long until she lost count of her steps from the snowbound car, each one hard-fought, but it couldn't have been more than thirty before she had to stop. Hunched over, she struggled to catch her breath with cold crisp gasps. The snow was knee-deep, and her energy had left her in the final few steps. Her breathing was now a heavy pant, with sweat stinging her eyes and dripping from her brows.

She growled at her inability to go on. What could she do? She had to be realistic and stop to catch her second wind, wiping her face with Phil's grubby apron that now hung loosely off her bump—she couldn't be bothered carrying it. Her feet were numb, and stamping them didn't help. They would probably be a lot worst if it wasn't for the clunky lumps of brown leather bolting her to the ground. Still, the boots were heavy, and she wondered if they helped or hindered. Probably the latter. Her progress hadn't been easy. With every step, it felt like some sort of magnetic force was pulling her soles deeper and harder into the frozen surface.

With a glance behind, she was surprised to see the lack of distance she'd made from the car. Disappointing, considering the effort she'd just put in. To her left and right, there was nothing but pine trees covered in snow, masking the wilderness beyond. At least the sky was crystal clear—a beautiful blue. The sun hung low, and she couldn't help but appreciate the beauty of the winter wonderland she found herself in. Stunning, like a Christmas advert, one that portrayed this white paradise in breathtaking fashion. But beneath her marvel, something wasn't right with the otherwise perfect scene.

A few feet off to her right—easily missed if you weren't looking—were the prints of something that had come out of the trees, stopped, then returned. She stepped closer and studied them, seeing that beneath the displaced snow they were clear, and unmistakably the track marks of a dog. A large dog at that, and *only* a dog's tracks. No boot prints accompanied them, indicating a wild animal's presence, or a stray? Her heart pounded as she realised that moments before she left the car, some sort of large dog had sauntered out of the trees. Her father's warning screamed through her head.

"Oh, no. Oh, no, no, no."

She looked around, then back to the trail, to where it veered off and disappeared behind a stand of large pines where the light didn't penetrate.

As she stood there, bewildered, the whole situation felt surreal. She'd been out for a Sunday drive with her man, and now here she was, snowbound and alone in an isolated valley in the Wicklow Mountains. How more fucked up could it be?

Or was she alone? Where the final paw print ended and the treeline began, something glowed. Two things. Eyes—golden eyes—staring right back at her.

They were narrow, with two jet-black pupils fixated on her. Frozen to the spot, she strained to see what lay below, squinting until she made out a long skinny snout and a plume of vapour that rose through the branches.

When the full realisation of what she was looking at hit her, she swallowed back the urge to run like hell away, remembering from somewhere deep in her past instructions never to run from a wild animal. She straightened up, fear coursing through her like ice-cold shards. A wolf. It was unmistakable. It was unreal. A dream? No, worse than a dream—a fucking nightmare.

She looked up and down the road in a desperate attempt to find something that might aid her, but all she could see was Phil's dirty uniform hanging off her and the vast white wilderness beneath the clear-blue sky. The beast had her in full view, there was no doubting that. The unwashed smell from her overalls now hit her hard, which meant the animal could smell it, too. She held back a whimper when she turned, locking eyes with what had to be one of those released grey wolves.

The shadows shifted within the trees and the breath-vapour increased. Her own breath caught and she thought she was going to have a heart attack with the sudden tightness. Had it moved? Why was it breathing so fast now? Then its snout appeared, clear as day, a string of steaming drool dangling from the side of its mouth.

"Fuck." she whispered, swallowing back the hardest ball of fear she'd ever experienced. Even with the cold, every hair on her body was electrified, with goosebumps erupting all over her.

Then it growled—a low rumble that turned her blood to ice. With a sudden shift, the beast lunged from the trees and powered through the snow, obviously intent on charging down its prey. Her.

With a terrified scream, she ran back the way she'd come as fast as she could. The car that seemed so close moments ago now looked to be miles away, with every step she took making no discernible difference. It was like she was one of those pitiful animals you see on nature shows—hunted in slow motion. The boots were holding her back. She tore them off and flung them with all her might at the wolf, who took a moment to sniff them before continuing on its deadly mission. As a result, she found better rhythm, managing to move through the snow by swinging out her legs—one arm held out for balance, the other cradling her bump to keep it from bouncing up and down. It was an awkward stride, yet somehow effective. At first, she couldn't hear a thing, but as she closed in on the car, the beast's growls and snarls grew louder, bearing down on her, and she was positive she could feel its hot breath against her neck. Adrenaline surged throughout her and her temples thumped from the rushing blood.

She glanced back as she ran, seeing the wolf skipping effortlessly across the top of the snow—its hind legs flicking white spray up with every stride, rapidly gaining speed and bridged the gap between them.

It was all about flight, never mind fight— no time to think of anything else. The car was her only hope. She reached the stranded Ford, her momentum slamming her up against the bonnet, forcing a frustrated groan out of her as she reached both hands out to prevent herself from falling.

She glanced over her left shoulder and saw nothing. Was it gone? Then she looked over her right shoulder and a massive ball of grey fur filled her view. She raised her hands without thinking, but the wolf lunged low and sank its teeth into her left calf, easily penetrating the two layers of clothing and punctured the skin. She screamed in pain—the sound echoing through the valley. The wolf let go, maybe thrown off by her response, but only for a moment before it dove back in and bit her leg a second time, just under the kneecap. Its powerful jaws clamped down and it shook its head from side to side in a frenzy that had Erin screaming again. It dragged her down in front of the car, her blood splashing onto the snow, melting it as soon as it made contact. She clawed at the icy ground, hoping to pull herself away, but it was useless.

For some reason, the wolf released its grip, took a step back, and snarled, seemingly unsure of its next move. Something from back in Erin's childhood flashed into her mind—a memory of sitting on the couch with her dad, watching one of his much-loved nature programmes—and it came to her that this wolf was displaying a lack of killing experience, maybe because it was young. The fucker was probably a renegade, out on its own.

Then it made a clumsy lunge, but she rolled to her left, onto her bump, and crawling forward as fast as she could towards the passenger door. But she wasn't fast enough and the wolf bit down again, this time on her ankle, its jaws locking tight. To her horror, it pulled at her, again and again, dragging her away from the car with powerful bursts of strength.

As it pulled and jerked, she got turned onto her back, then onto her front, then onto her back again. Her vision blurred as it shifted from white snow to pine trees to blue sky, like she was stuck in some sort of tumble dryer. The beast's strength was overwhelming, and, as it was, she felt powerless to combat it.

But something sparked inside—something silent and strong—and in an act of desperate defiance, she lashed out with her free foot and kicked the beast hard in the face, stunning it enough to release its hold on her. But for only a second. It snarled and snotted at her before lunging in again with its jaws wide open.

She thought it would go for her leg again, but this time it aimed for a fatal blow at her neck, and she just managed to avoid its teeth with an instinctive jerk, its hot breath and saliva hitting her skin as she moved, rolling onto her baby bump. Then she spotted the apron laid out where she first fell in front of the car. Her survival instincts kicked in again and she grabbed it and turned to face the oncoming wolf.

The beast, its eyes full of mad aggression, stamped and growled as it angled itself towards her neck again, it's deathly intention unmistakeable.

Erin put all her energy behind her next action and flung the apron out, somehow managing to wrap it around the wolf's head, evoking crazed kicks and bucks, snarls and roars in its attempts to pull free. It was all she needed—valuable seconds to allow her scramble to her feet.

The wolf fought to remove the smock, its growls turning into frustrated yelps. This hadn't been part of its plan. Erin limped around to the side of the car and pulled the door open, and in that moment when she paused for breath, the wolf got loose.

It looked around, spotted her, and wasted no time in charging towards its prey, but she scrambled into the car and pulled the door shut, locking herself into what she hoped was a safe space.

The wolf growled and snarled at her through the passenger window, slamming against the glass in an attempt to get at her, even ramming its head against it to break it, but without success.

Erin, overwhelmed with terror, screamed with every move the beast made. The golden eyes glared in at her with a determined focus, its breath fogging up the glass. She shook and cried, in an equal mixture of horror and relief. The fucker hadn't got her. She'd survived, with her baby. The beast had failed. That knowledge brought more tears, because she knew it wasn't over—not by a longshot.

She leaned over and pressed down hard on the car horn to scare the animal off, but with every beep, the wolf just howled—the sound only fuelling its anger.

It started walking around the front of the car, from left to right and back again, always staring in at her, its focus never wavering—and that low growl, a constant sound from behind its bloodied jaws. Erin held onto the steering wheel and watched it, horrified, but also fascinated. The beast was making a point—it was the hunter and she was the prey, and all that kept them apart was a thin sheet of glass. The more she looked at it, the more convinced she was that this wolf wouldn't stop until it got what it wanted. Her.

NINE

With darkness pushing in from the back of her mind, she just about managed to compose herself. Shaking, terrified, and alone, she pulled the one bit of brightness out of the horror: the beast outside could do nothing to her now, and this allowed her time to gather her thoughts. Why was it on its own? Solo. Most unusual for an animal that normally hunted in packs. She didn't know a whole lot but that much was for sure. And she could thank her father for that as well. As she watched it, pacing to and fro, she noted that it looked underweight, but then again, she'd never seen a wolf in the flesh before, apart from the ones in Dublin Zoo, so her basis for comparison was grounded purely on guesswork.

Getting over onto the backseat was a struggle, but she needed to stretch out her leg and assess the damage. Again, she let the back of her seat down, then up again once she was over. Her heart was still pounding from all the adrenaline, and she noticed that Phil's chef jacket was soaked through, most likely from all the snow, but also from the cold sweat that covered her. She trembled as she removed the blood-drenched trousers, slowly revealing her wounded leg—the skin, pale like snow where it wasn't smeared in blood. Horrific. She couldn't help gasping at the sight, hot tears running down her cheeks. What a mess. And surreal to look at—she'd never seen anything like it, and found it difficult to believe she was looking at her own leg. It reminded her of a scene from one of her dad's World War Two movies where the allies got blasted out of it on a French beach. Daddy loved to watch them at Christmas time, which is why the images stuck so firmly in her memory.

Her crotch was soaking wet. Piss? Sweat? Not blood, anyway, which was such a relief. She stripped down to her underwear and hung the garments on the back of the front seats to air out. Shivers and shakes ran ragged through her and she did her best to combat the convulsions by wrapping her arms around herself and squeezing.

Her left leg had been mangled pretty badly, with blood oozing from the deeper wounds. Sizable gashes and lacerations ran from the ankle to her knee, but the shock was still keeping the worst of the pain at bay, for now. She reached for the chef trousers and tore small stripes up the frittered leg. At least the wolf had made it easier to rip. She wrapped the makeshift bandages around the wounds, and while her hands shook with every movement and her grip was weak, she managed to finish, and it seemed to do the trick, though blood still seeped through in places.

The pain was beginning to register now. The wolf growled again at the window behind her head—the smell of blood sending it into rapture.

She turned to look out at the beast but was halted by a sharp stabbing pain that shot up her back.

"What the fuck? No! No, no, no." Blood and mucus were leaking through her underwear and onto the car seat. That was the smell the wolf had caught, and now it slammed against the door, its howling beyond frenzy.

The animal's instincts knew before she did.

"Fuck, no, this can't be happening. Seriously? Not now. Please, not now!" she screamed in a blind panic, and with that the cramps intensified, the pain crippling her lower back.

The pathway that led to isolation, now revealed a portal where a void might soon be filled with light.

TEN

Two hours into the labour and Erin was almost wishing for death to take the pain away, or at the very least, an epidural to free her from the agony and allow her to control her breathing, which had become a mix of choking gawps and deep lifesaving breaths.

Her injured leg had grown numb—almost void of feeling compared to the intense cramping that twisted and stirred within her belly. She tried her hardest to remain focused and count the contractions, but the whole ordeal was so overwhelming, and at times she found herself screaming for a midwife, Phil, or anyone at all to come help her. Each time she screamed, the wolf howled behind her, bringing her back to the realisation that she was alone and had pretty much been induced by the beast.

The pain and trauma fought to override her rational thinking, but she pushed against it with all her might. This was happening and she had to deal with it, here and now, because if she were to take the luxury of focusing on the black dots dancing in front of her eyes and ended up passing out, then she could wake up to find her baby had been lost. She knew this. It wasn't about her anymore—simple as that. Her mothering instinct had kicked in, and the situation and the leg injury no longer mattered. The wolf outside didn't matter. Phil's absence didn't matter. Nothing else mattered. All that counted now was getting this situation under control and birthing this baby as safely as she could.

She began by controlling her breathing, or at least trying her best to. Deep cold breaths in through her nose, hold, then out through her mouth. She cast back to the antenatal classes she and Phil took, remembering the doula's advice on how she should enjoy the birthing experience. Jesus Christ, never in a million years did she think she'd be having a baby in the back of Phil's banger of a car. Phil, where was he now? It was hard to forget his lack of interest and mockery of the whole process, showing up late to appointments and complaining that he had to put his hand in his pocket to attend classes led by a woman he described as a *fucking hippy*.

His attitude infuriated her, especially now, but she refused to get hung up on him. He hadn't bothered then so it didn't matter if he was here now or not, despite his overwhelming desire to have a son.

She sat up as best she could on the backseat and prepared herself. The wolf howled and she slapped the window and roared out at him. She grabbed the chef jacket and flattened it out across the seat, then tossed what remained of the trousers onto the front passenger seat and cleared space to make room for her to lie in the most comfortable way possible.

Sweat covered her, stinging her eyes and rolling down the sides of her face as the pressure increased and her baby came closer and closer to entering the world. She reached down and felt around the entrance to her vagina, admitting to herself that it would have to be guesswork to determine when to start pushing, focusing on the pressure because she had no way of knowing how far her cervix was dilated.

The pain shooting up her back made it difficult to move, the strain spreading across her shoulders. With every scream she released, she sensed her body preparing for the ordeal. It was then she realised that after the baby was out, there would still be work to do. She remembered the doula talk about the afterbirth and the cutting of the chord. That was the only part of the course Phil expressed interest in and it was supposed to be his job on the day. Today. But without him around, she would have to do it herself.

Then the realisation hit her that she'd left Phil's knives in the boot. She screamed out in frustration. Why in the hell hadn't she taken them in with the boots and uniform? No way in the world could she get out again, not with that monster waiting on her. Young or not, he'd have her before she got the boot open.

"Fuck." She kicked the door. "Come on!" She grabbed the back of the seat and kicked the door again. "Why didn't you think, you stupid woman?"

She was about to kick out again when she felt something hard just behind the top of the seat. What the...? Then it came to her, and she actually let out a joyous whoop that had the wolf howling again.

"Are you fucking serious, Erin?"

She sat up, fully focused, the panic of the situation banished to the background as she kicked into auto pilot, allowed her mind to detach from her horrific reality.

Not sure how the seat released, she sat up a bit more and took a look, the wolf jumping up at the window when it seen her. It could jump all it liked at this stage—she had her mission, and nothing was going to get in her way. Once she shifted back, the seat dropped down easy enough, the stink coming through from Phil's rotten leftovers. All she could do was breath through her mouth—otherwise she'd be puking up again.

She wasn't able to bend enough to look inside, so she reached in instead and felt around until she caught hold of the shoulder strap of Phil's gym bag. With a deep breath, she pulled it through. Okay, let's do this. She rummaged around inside but couldn't find the knives. What the hell had she done with them? She found deodorant, aftershave, shower gel, clean socks, boxer shorts—the usual stuff Phil brought to work with him. But no fucking knives.

Then she saw it...

It was like all her Christmas's had come early. She lifted the medium-sized bottle of whiskey from the inside pocket. A *shoulder* her father would say. Unopened and still in a brown-paper bag, it was an unusual item to have with his work things, but Phil was drinking a lot more lately so she supposed it made some sort of sense.

Without hesitation, she uncapped the bottle, the plastic twisting free with a satisfying click.

Jameson. Two large mouthfuls burned into her chest, warmed her tummy, and sent an almost euphoric glow through her. When she inhaled the smoky smell of hops, a delicious shiver raced from the tips of her toes all the way up to her head. This was brilliant, and just what she needed.

She took one more gulp, let it settle, capped the bottle, then reached back into the stinking boot. The knives had to be in there somewhere. It didn't take long to find them, and she pulled them out onto her lap for inspection. She had what she needed now, so wasted no time in lifting the back of the seat back into place. So good not to have that stench in her face.

Over the next minute or so, she gathered her thoughts and placed everything she was going to need around her. The edge of the blades gleamed brightly after a wipe from an alcohol-soaked sock – Sterilisation and being drunk – the first item in every medic's pack when at war, her father used to say. Next, she stretched her legs out, then went back inside her mind and focused on the task at hand.

She would let it happen at its own pace, but as she waited, time seemed to pass so slow every minute felt like an eternity.

As the pressure mounted, she felt sure it was time to start pushing. She positioned herself along the back seat, placed one ankle up on the back of the driver's seat, bracing it as best she could under the headrest—the pain from her wounds barely registering among the pain between her legs. Then she wrapped the seatbelt around her other ankle, hoisted it up, and secured it around the rear headrest.

With her legs elevated and secured into place, she took another mouthful of whiskey. She checked her position one last time and placed the small, blue-handled fillet knife up on the canvas boot cover behind the rear headrests.

It was time. Fuck, it was time. With all her might, she pushed. Her screams reverberated off the windows, sending the wolf into another howling frenzy. With every push, her body drained of energy, but she willed herself on and it wasn't too long before she felt the baby crowning.

Even so, an age passed and the baby didn't move any further, which brought on another flush of panic. She felt around, flinching when she touched the child's head, and groaned when she realised the poor thing was stuck. This was where she needed her midwife to confirm her suspicions. But with no one around to assist, she was left with no choice but to take matters into her own hands. She took hold of the knife. Her hands shook so much she thought she wouldn't be able to do it, but she took a couple of deep breaths, and then, as if in slow motion, she reached down, using her fingertips to guide the point of the blade to the spot between the baby's head and the rim of her vulva.

She took a deep breath, closed her eyes and, with a quick downward flick, cut against herself.

The rough episiotomy created an instant release. Her autopilot reactivated and, with the deepest breath she ever took in her life, she pushed with every ounce of strength she had left in her exhausted body, screaming like a banshee out of hell as she did so.

Then it happened—the baby's head and torso burst through. She grabbed the infant by the skull, gasped, then pulled and pushed at the same time.

Within seconds, the baby was out. Born.

Silence, not even the wolf making a sound.

Between her sobs, she pulled the child up to her chest and gave it an open-handed tap on the back. The impact had immediate effect, causing the baby to gasp and then cry—little squeals that lifted Erin's heart as high as it could get.

Overcome with joy, she grabbed the chef jacket and wrapped the child in it as best she could. Then she used one of Phil's clean socks to wipe blood and fluids from its mouth and nose, before cradling the baby to her—an instant rush of love bringing more tears. Mother and child rested back and cuddled, but she knew there was still work to do.

She eased open the chef jacket, lifted the knife, and cut the umbilical cord, leaving enough to be able to tie off. Shattered, she wrapped the child again and placed it on the passenger seat. The wolf was still moving about outside, growling now and again, but it hadn't howled in a good while. Maybe it sensed what was happening. Fuck it, she didn't have time to dwell on it. She lay back and started pushing again, running her hands over her belly in slow arcs to assist. The afterbirth didn't take long to come, and she found the ordeal easier than expected. She cut it free and dumped it onto the driver's seat. Then she took a moment to process what she'd just been through.

All she wanted to do was sleep, but even through her exhaustion, she couldn't help but feel proud of what she'd just accomplished. She took another large mouthful of whiskey in celebration, relishing its internal heat, then proceeded to tend her birth wounds, using a pair of Phil's socks as a seal. She pulled on his boxer shorts, which were tight, and would hopefully hold the makeshift dressing in place.

The baby was quiet but seemed fine. She placed it on the back seat and released it from the chef coat, which she put on herself, taking the time also to get back into the tattered uniform trousers—her jeans were not an option, too tight to consider.

Her body was void of energy now, and all she wanted was to rest. She lifted the baby and lay back, placing it across her chest, running her hands over every part of its body, which is when she noticed that it was a boy.

No more speculation now—the result was confirmed.

She smiled from ear to ear, then wept from the overwhelming emotion. He was the most beautiful baby she had ever seen. His face was red and stressed from the birth, his skull a bit out of shape, but none of that mattered—he was alive and well, and nuzzled into her, his touch filling her with so much love. She could make out some of her own and some of Phil's features—her eyes and lips, Phil's nose. She wanted to name him there and then but couldn't think of anything on the spot. Fuck it, she was just happy he was safe and here with her now.

The baby took to the nipple with ease and began suckling. Erin zoned out and lay back. She knew what was ahead of her but decided to take some time to recoup much-needed strength.

As she rested, she knew that time was working against her. With her injuries and loss of blood, she had no choice but to get herself and her baby boy to safety. Beyond the relative security of the car lay danger and salvation, and her need for one over the other would hopefully save her from sinking into the abyss.

ELEVEN

As the afternoon progressed, and Erin and baby slumbered, the sun glided across the sky, almost without being noticed, but she was thankful for its constant presence. It gave her a sense of security that she wouldn't have if she remained here after dark. Nearly the whole day had gone by and no one had come to help her off this mountain. No helicopter, no search party, and no sign of her father, not to mention her missing fiancé. Where the hell was Philip?

The wolf hadn't made its presence heard for some time, but she didn't doubt that it was in the vicinity, watching and waiting—biding its time. She had to accept her situation, and needed to prepare to exit this nightmare and escape on foot before night fell. It didn't help that she had to wear Phil's filthy garments. The smell was almost unbearable, but she had no choice if both of them were to survive.

The baby was fine, wrapped in a pair of crinkled but dry t-shirts she'd found balled up at the bottom of the bag. The bag itself had become his first carry cot. It wasn't ideal, but would have to do, and would allow her use her arms to keep balanced out on the road. She looked out all the windows, taking time to examine if the coast was clear. The animal wouldn't be far. After all, she was easy prey in its eyes.

The two rear windows were roll-down—manually operated—clearly a cost-saving measure by the manufacturer. She went to the driver's side and opened the window a couple of inches. The ice around the rim cracked as the glass moved and a cold but fresh breeze flowed in, much to the dismay of the baby, who cried as he experienced his first winter air.

She comforted him until he settled, then whistled out the window to coax the hungry beast over. No response. It had to be close by, but she couldn't see any fresh tracks beyond the trail it had worn around the car. The silence was eerie, the shadows of the trees stretching across the road, forming haunting silhouettes on the snow.

Without warning, the beast lunged at the gap in the window, the car rocking with the force of its attack. Erin acted with pure instinct and whacked the animal across its snout, forcing a yelp and recoil. Much snarling and gnashing followed.

She figured it was as hungry as her, and probably as desperate, but this time, while fear ate into her, from deep inside, the mothering and survival instincts were in control and brewing up a storm.

The gap wasn't big enough for what she wanted, so she rolled the window down a bit more and waited, pulling the gym bag closer. The wolf didn't lunge this time, maybe sensing something wasn't right. It continued snarling as it shifted from side to side, never taking its eyes off Erin.

Keeping an eye on the animal, she used Phil's blue knife to cut several small pieces from the placenta, two of which she tossed out the small slit in the window.

The wolf was on them in a second, devouring them in a vicious frenzy.

"I got you now, you bastard," she shouted out. "Liked that, did you? Here, have some more."

She tossed a bigger piece farther out and prepared to execute the plan. Not just any plan, but *the* plan, which she'd cooked up over the afternoon and was praying would work. With the wolf distracted on the driver's side, she retreated back and opened the passenger-side door.

It opened easy, now that the snow around the car had been walked over by herself and the wolf. The baby remained silent, as if wise to what was going on. His shadowed eyes looked up at her from the bag, and her heart melted at the strength of their connection.

She raised one of her blood-soaked fingers to her lips and settled him with a gentle hush. It was time for a gamble—one she had no choice taking if they weren't to perish in this isolated nightmare. She slipped out and placed bag and baby on the roof, then got back in and tossed another piece of her afterbirth out the window for the wolf to gobble up. The beast obliged, darting after it to hoover up the delicacy.

Happy enough with that, she rolled down the window a little more. In an instant, the wolf lunged, sticking its snout and two front paws through the gap, snarling and snapping as it tried to force its way into the car. The animal's weight and power pushed the window down and within seconds it had half its body in, forcing Erin to recoil, shrieking and screaming at it in return.

She stared at it for a moment, her breath coming hard, then she pulled the remaining placenta from the front seat and threw it at the beast. With a lifeless thud, the organ landed in front of the crazed animal, who didn't hesitate, its teeth sinking right in—it growled so loud the noise struck terror into Erin.

Without a moment to lose—the situation was way too dangerous and she was barely in control of it—she waited for the wolf to focus on its food one more time, and in the split-second the beast took its eyes off her, she plunged Phil's large black knife into the animal's neck.

With a howl, the beast jumped and bucked, attempting to bite the blade, which was now deeply lodged, with dark blood spurting from the wound.

Erin grabbed the handle and pulled it out, the wolf reacting as if stabbed again. Then she screamed for all she was worth and stabbed the animal two more times. Blood shot out, the hot liquid splashing her face and spreading down the animal's coat.

When she dropped the knife and reversed out the passenger door, the wolf tried to follow, but she used her whole body and slammed the door shut, trapping the wounded beast inside, for now.

The plan had worked, but she was all too aware of the open window on the other side. She scrambled to her feet, grabbed the bag with the baby snug inside off the roof, and took herself away in the same direction Phil had taken the day before.

The wounded wolf howled and whimpered behind her, the harrowing sound echoing across the valley.

Erin limped and struggled on, the bag underarm, its handles slung over her shoulder. She was fit, but she had to stop to catch her breath, her energies depleted, not only from having her leg savaged, but giving birth.

Her heart nearly stopped when the wolf scrambled through the open window. It stopped, panting, watching her. Then it moved towards her, its head down, obviously weakened by its wounds.

Fear threatened to overcome her, its power crippling as it surged through her body. The animal snarled. Even in the light, its eyes glowed as they fixed on her and her baby. She couldn't move, her muscles refusing to obey her silent and desperate commands to flee. It continued on, and she was about to scream when she noticed that every step it took was slower and limper than the last. Behind it, a thick trail of blood pitted the snow. As it came to within a few feet, it stopped, scratched its neck where blood still gushed, then collapsed.

Erin edged towards it, keeping herself between it and her baby. When she stood over the mass of grey and black fur, she looked it in the eye.

The wolf looked back, pulled back its mouth—possibly in one last effort to prove its Alpha worth—then its light faded. Its final breath, a long exhalation, came with a low whimper that was the last thing she expected from a savage wolf.

She almost pitied it, but that soon transformed into a sense of victory—one she wanted to celebrate—but before that she had to make sure the result was final. With great caution, she tapped her foot against its snout.

No reaction, no sound. Nothing.

Something flashed beneath the fur around its neck. Something metallic. She knew the blade hadn't snapped, so it couldn't be that. Using her foot again, she flicked at the object, revealing the source—a collar.

There were no ownership details on the tag, but it had the Irish Wolf Conservation logo and some sort of number engraved. A sharp chill ran up her back. Did the animal escape? If not, then where was she? Surely Phil wouldn't be stupid enough to lead them into such a dangerous place as the sectioned-off area? Her temples pounded, and all she could do was close her eyes, take deep breaths, and try to control the panic.

When she re-opened her eyes, disbelief overwhelmed her. What the fuck? The animal was...changing—its form shifting—the snout retracted, revealing human-like eyes that carried a dull lifeless gaze. Its limbs morphed, too, to resemble that of a human, and before she could fully grasp what was happening, the carcass revealed itself to be a mix of wolf and man. And not just any man—a familiar mongrel of a man, naked, with thick grey and black hair in patches all over. Geoff fucking Baron.

She gasped at the sight before her. What the hell had just happened? Geoff Baron was supposed to be in Canada, off the grid. And werewolves where fictional creatures, weren't they? Obviously not, because this monster was lying in front of her. Then a horrific dawning crept through her. If this thing hadn't escaped— if she was within the reservation—that meant there were more of them. More wolf-men hybrids. The thought shook her to the core. She had no choice but to get moving. One werewolf had nearly been the death of her. A pack would be another matter altogether.

TWELVE

Cries of hunger pierced her ears and bounced off both sides of the valley, but she couldn't stop to attend to him. Her mothering autopilot was all that fuelled her now—the same determination that gave her the strength to drag herself across the snowy valley. The sun had yet to fully set, its last rays fading behind the horizon. It wouldn't be long before the night crept in and took its place.

She'd left the werewolf in her wake, shaking the mental reality out of her head, or at least she was trying too. Geoff Baron, Phil's best friend, was a werewolf. Crazy, mad, but real, and the bastard had almost had her, and her baby. And who was to say there weren't more out there? Was Geoff the only...thing of its kind? Did it mean the other wolves in her father's sanctuary were also werewolves? That stopped her in her tracks. Her father's sanctuary. Did her father know what was out there? Is that what he'd tried to warn her about? Did he know about Geoff Baron?

She pushed it out of her head and continued on. Phil had said the nearest village was only forty minutes away. Easy for him—in her state of health, *only* forty minutes would seem like a lifetime. As it was, she could barely place weight on her leg, reduced to dragging it after her through the snow. Blood still leaked from the wounds and her checkered bandaging was soaked through. It felt like an eternity covering any discernible distance, but she summoned strength from somewhere deep inside and continued to move along, taking handfuls of snow to quench her thirst.

The infant cried a harrowing wail, and she tried her best to sooth him, but it was a waste of time. The boy was cold and hungry, and she needed to get him off this road and somewhere warm to feed and comfort him.

Her thoughts jumped to Phil and how he'd failed to return last night. Anger surged and she wished something nasty had happened to him, because if he didn't have a legitimate excuse for not coming back, she felt well within her rights to do him harm. She nearly laughed at the thought of his face at the news that his best buddy was a fucking werewolf. A dead werewolf. And where was her father? Despite his warnings and concerns, he hadn't shown, either—it had been almost twenty-four hours since she'd spoken to him.

But, she supposed, none of that mattered now. She'd survived her abandonment alone and delivered her baby boy without any assistance. And he was alive and safe in his bag as she dragged herself through this Siberian-esque landscape.

THIRTEEN

Just as she was gaining in confidence, feeling like she was making real progress along the grim path, her good leg shuddered, with all strength draining out of it like someone had pulled a plug. As much as she tried to remain standing, her legs went out from under her and she collapsed in the middle of the road. She caught the bag before it hit the snow, but the jostling had the child crying again. All she could do was pull the bag tight to her and shush the baby, but the poor thing was beyond comforting. Exhausted, she lay defeated in the cold and miserable slush, looking up at the darkening sky as a flock of birds flew overhead. They had dark feathers, so she assumed they were crows. Maybe they were ducks and she was delirious—she didn't know—it was hard to tell with everything spinning. Another flock sailed overhead in motionless flight. This time she was sure they were ducks. Could they see her?

Time stood still. She envied them their freedom.

The full moon had dark cloud cutting into it, revealing a white fishhook against the night sky. She held her whimpering baby in close after pulling him out of the bag. His face crunched up into a frown. He was uncomfortable and unable to say so. His only form of communication was a high-pitched wail that pierced her eardrums again.

"I'm sorry, baby," she whispered in a soft, shaky voice. "I'm sorry you had to come into this world this way." A quiver gripped her bottom lip and tears blurred her vision. Beneath the shivers racking her body, a numbness was creeping in and taking hold. Drained of energy, she was unable to pick herself up. She looked at her boy. "Your dada wanted to call you Philip Junior. Did you know that? But I don't think you are like him." She blinked the tears away. "I'm sorry, baba. I'm... I'm not sure if I can get up and keep going."

In her desperate state, the infant's cries faded into the murk, almost not registering with her, as if he'd slipped away into the distance.

Was she shutting down? It felt like it. The blood loss. It had to be that. As much as she didn't want to give in and die, her body was telling her that this was the hand she'd been dealt, and the dealer didn't accept refunds. She clutched the baby tighter. Her breath was shallower now, slower—each one a struggle. She closed her eyes in anticipation of what must be the crossover into the next world, listening to her rasping pants—the sound a gentle backdrop to the oncoming void.

Something her mother once said came to her: when someone is dying, their mind leaves their body and the most beautiful music will play and help usher the lost soul into the next world.

She opening her eyes and listened for that sound, but the only response was silence. The cold had gripped every part of her, with exhaustion anchoring her to the freezing ground. Giving in to the overwhelming shivers, she kissed the child on the forehead and closed her eyes.

"Bye, bye, baba."

FOURTEEN

As she sailed across the blackened plains, snowflakes sprinkled through the weightless, desolate silence. Stars sparkled like eyes, welcoming her to the other side of the astral bridge, drawing her closer, pulling her down. But it wasn't right, she should have been rising, not falling, not feeling, not sensing beyond herself.

Sounds of the night came to her. The woods were alive—footfalls, shifting the tiniest pine needles beneath the snow, crackling as if they were the driest of twigs. Snow fell from branches when brushed against, as if in cascade, but silent to the rest of the world. Their breaths came to her, with each movement a communication of intent, their mission clear, forcing her back to life, as if a shot of adrenaline had been pumped into her heart. Her eyes shot open and she struggled to clear her vision—to her left and right. They were coming. And she knew. It was as if her senses had sharpened beyond expectation.

She didn't have to speculate on what was coming for her. They were in her mind, clear as day, at least six or seven of them, drawn by the smell of her bloodstained clothes, or the baby's cries. Perhaps both. And revenge. Yes, they were hungry for revenge. They were closing in, and this time she knew she wouldn't stand a chance. Her position was wide open, and to say she was vulnerable would be the understatement of the year. They would tear her and the baby apart in seconds and, with that very thought, another surge of energy shot through her like a bolt of lightning from Zeus himself.

Once she struggled to her feet, she hoisted the bag onto her shoulder. The boy cried, but she didn't care, motivated purely once again by her survival mode. She looked ahead—the road still covered in snow and seemingly leading to nowhere. Her focus came easier now, and it took no effort to see that the way ahead slanted downhill, and she knew this could be to her advantage, if she could get moving.

The wolves weren't visible yet, but she saw them in her mind, off to either side of the road, in the cover of the trees. She didn't need to remember her father's documentaries to know that the pack leader would be coordinating the attack.

A howl broke the silence and the hairs on her neck and arms shot up. They were communicating—hunting in an organised manner—but from where and when the attack would come, she didn't know. Probably why they were the hunters and she was the prey, and if she didn't pick up the pace, it was *game over*.

Something up ahead caught her attention, but she couldn't quite make it out. Whatever it was, it stretched across the road.

As she got closer, dragging her leg, her energy ebbing, the object became clearer. She stopped, not believing what she saw. A fence. A freestanding, chain-linked fence, blocked the road.

The wolves went quiet. She looked around her, knowing the attack was imminent.

The boy cried.

She pushed forward, groaning with the madness of it, head down, battling on, not giving up. Then, without warning, she crashed into the fence and screamed for help through the links. Beyond was nothing but empty white road.

She looked back up the hill, her gaze darting in all directions, but all she could see was grey wilderness—no wolves, no attack, and no footprints other than her own. Her breath rasped from the enormous effort it took to get to the fence.

Did she imagine the sounds? Had delirium overtaken her once again?

She examined the fence and the surrounding area. Just beyond it, on the side of the road, was a sign:

ROAD CLOSED

Below that was another sign:

DESIGNATED HUNTING GROUND. PRACTICE EXTREME CAUTION.

Fuck!

Against the night sky were lights from what she assumed to be the nearest village, glowing in an amber haze, like a dome over the area. The fence was so high, and she shook it with her free hand, praying for the first sign of life to appear. Razor wire ran along the top of it, making it impossible to climb over. She realised without looking back that her mind hadn't played tricks on her and her ordeal was far from over. They were coming for her. She scanned the area. To her left, she counted three, with four on her right.

Cold sweat prickled across her back. They were bearing down on her—her body was telling her, and it wasn't able for any form of defence. The lights were too far away, making a call for help useless, and the fencing accomplished its job of keeping the wolves and their prey inside the compound. Tears came at the thought of being so close to safety, and after everything she'd been through.

She considered throwing the baby over the fence, but it was too high. Instead, she fell to her knees and placed him under her body. It was the only thing she could do.

The wolves surrounded her.

She looked up to see what she assumed to be the Alpha male staring at her. The beast was huge—twice the size of the one she'd killed. Its dark yellow eyes glared at her from above its long snout, the whiskers lifting as it revealed its terrifying teeth. It tilted its head down, signalling for its pack members to launch their attack. Erin tucked herself in and waited for the end.

At first, there was a loud bang, followed by a squeal. A second bang came a moment later, and Erin jolted on the spot. She looked around to see the two lead wolves hitting the ground in front of her, snow puffing around them.

Her gaze darted from side to side as she tried to comprehend what had happened. The remaining animals were as confused as her.

Two more bangs thundered in her ears, and the wolves whined and retreated, reluctant to leave their fallen behind. One more bang had them scarpering off beyond the treeline, well out of sight.

Erin sat up in a daze. Against the backdrop of moonlight, two tall silhouettes approached. As they drew closer, she noticed through her tears that one was wearing a sleeveless black Gillet and held a rifle, muzzle up. The other man looked to be a Garda, his Hi-Viz jacket visible beyond anything else but the moon. They were calling to her, but it sounded like someone speaking while she was under water. And she wanted to reply, but fatigue wouldn't allow her to utter a single word, leaving the men standing on the other side of the fence gesturing and shouted down to her.

***

She drifted in and out of consciousness. In brief flashes of awareness, she came to see that she was lying in the back of a truck, wrapped in blankets, her head elevated on a makeshift pillow of rough material that itched her face. Voices filtered in from outside—garbled words, as if through walkie-talkies. The smell of gunpowder was all around her. Then she noticed the road through the slit in the dark cotton curtain draped over the back of the truck.

Next time she woke to cries. Blue lights flashed, and the curtain had been pulled aside. Her stomach lurched when she saw a female Guard outside holding what she assumed was her baby. The boy, wrapped in a blanket, was being walked around—the officer struggling to sooth the hungry child, whose squeals everyone knew about.

The interior of the truck spun and her eyes rolled back as she faded in and out of her darkness, her mind struggling to process everything that was happening.

"Help is on the way, miss," a man with a thick country accent called in to her. "Stay strong in there." It was the man in the Gillet. He wore a concerned smile.

She could only respond with groans.

He frowned, his mouth opening to reveal a set of bad teeth. A patch on his arm had a wolf emblem on it, with *Greene Security Group* underneath.

A paramedic climbed in and sat beside her. "Hello miss. What's your name?" He was young, and eager to help. "What is your name?" he asked again.

Erin was unable to engage—the darkness clouding her senses again. She could barely feel the medic attending to her leg.

"She's lost a lot of blood."

A sharp pain shot up her spine and she rolled onto her back and stared up at the dark canopy. The voices and sounds faded again, and she felt herself turning inward against the distant cries of her baby.

PART THREE

FIFTEEN

As the fog of sleep dissipated, Erin squinted and blinked against the harsh lighting above. The smell of disinfectant pinched her nostrils. Everything was a blur, but she persevered until things cleared up enough to see where she was. A hospital ward. The three beds opposite were empty, their curtains drawn back. A large window at the far end reflected back the room's light with a mirrored fade.

Then it came to her. She was in a Hospital, and by the looks of it, the place was in dire need of a paint job.

Her mouth was bone dry, her throat raw. She remained silent, unmoving as she took stock of her situation. The blue blanket over her was raised at the end. Her leg. Of course.

How could she forget that? She blinked a few more times, allowing visuals in. It was all a bit murky, but patches materialised. The doctors had worked through the night to save her life, giving credit to her strong spirit in assisting them in their struggle to prevent her succumbing to her trauma. They'd told her so when she came out of the anaesthetic. She'd had several units of blood during the operation, which lasted almost nine hours as they worked on her lower leg. They assured her they'd be able to rebuild the parts she'd lost, too badly damaged by the Geoff's tearing jaws. It would be a long-term recovery, with extensive grafting and physiotherapy, but they assured her she'd walk again, though probably with a limp.

They'd patched up and dressed her self-inflicted vaginal wound, placing her on two intravenous antibiotics to fight infection, which meant she wouldn't be able to breastfeed her baby.

"My baby!"

She shot up in the bed, or as much as the pain in her abdomen would allow.

"He's safe, dear," a woman with a soft-spoken voice said beside her. Erin flinched — she hadn't realised someone was sitting beside her. A nurse, with *Kelly* engraved on her name badge. She was young, with a lot of make-up around the eyes, her red hair tied back in a neat bun.

"But, where...?" Her words croaked—her tongue dry as sandpaper.

"He's on another ward," the nurse said, laying a warm hand on Erin's arm. "And he's fine. Just needed feeding and rest. You'll see him in time, but for now, you must rest as well and try to recoup your strength." She got up and tucked the blankets in around Erin, leaving her arms on top.

Erin didn't argue. Even if she wanted to, she hadn't the strength. She was still exhausted.

The nurse offered her a glass of water.

She took a sip and swished it around before swallowing, grimacing as her throat protested, but she took another, keeping the refreshing liquid in her mouth for longer, letting it get in everywhere. The tubes from the intravenous drip above her connected into twin ports in her right arm, taped up to prevent dislodgement. She wouldn't be doing anything to disturb the process. The last thing she wanted was infection setting in.

The nurse placed the glass on the bedside locker. "I believe you have a visitor waiting outside. We couldn't let him in until we knew you were well enough to see him. He was very insistent about seeing you, but the doctor was adamant that your rest was more important."

She checked her watch clipped to her breast pocket. "What do you think, Erin? You strong enough for a visit?"

"How long has he been waiting?" she asked. Even after the water, the words burned her throat.

"Maybe an hour."

She grimaced again as she swallowed, then nodded.

"No problem, dear, I'll send him in." She winked before she turned to leave.

Everything was so quiet in the empty ward. She rubbed her eyes, still tired, but her vision was clear. The cream walls were in bits. The floor was a mix of dark green and brown lino and had been recently mopped, if the shine and smell was anything to go by. A framed pictured of a pope hung over the entrance. Which pope, she didn't know, or care. Each bed was neatly made, with the drawn curtains opening up the room. A television set hung from a bracket in the far corner, a red dot signalling it was in standby mode.

Voices filtered in from outside, and trolleys moving about, but it was low-level and respectful noise, confirming her assumption that it was night. She should have taken note of the nurse's watch.

To the right of the window, a door had been left ajar—most likely the bathroom. The sight of it brought a cold jab from her bladder, telling her in no uncertain terms that it required attention. She took a deep breath and turned onto her side, then pushed herself up enough to be able to lean forward and pull the end of the blanket up. Just as she thought, they'd left a frame over her leg. She lifted it off and manoeuvred her legs over the side of the bed. Whatever painkillers she was on, they were having the desired effect, but it didn't prevent her feeling stiffness throughout her whole body. Her toes barely tipped the lino. The leg was heavily bandaged beneath a modern-looking Velcro splint. She smiled, relieved to see the limb in a clean, sanitised state. A positive start, and it boded well for a good recovery.

The floor was freezing, but nothing like the ice and snow she'd come out of. She put all her weight on her good foot, taking hold of the drip stand to ease away from the bed into a standing position. To her surprise, she was able to balance well enough. No way was she going to test her bandaged leg, though. She'd just lean on the stand and drag the injured limb along, like she'd done from the car to the fence.

While she could stand with assistance, she was still weak. Her good knee trembled, and her thigh actually quivered, the vibrations running through her pelvis, reminding her again how much she needed to piss. Would her good leg buckle and take her to the floor? Fuck it, the wolf hadn't beaten her, so a few shakes would hardly be a problem.

She took her time with each step, making the most of the steel IV rack as she wheeled it along. With a struggle and much thought, she was able to maneuverer her hospital gown out of the way while she went to the toilet.

The burning sensation was excruciating. They'd left a gap to enable urination, but the wound was oozing a bloody mucus that seeped through the dressing. She wiped beads of sweat from her forehead with the back of her hand, sure she felt the stitching shift from the pressure while she pissed. The effort. Christ. She closed her eyes and watched flashes of her nightmare come at her again. So clear. But despite the horror, she managed to crack a smile at the thought that she'd survived and given birth to her little boy. By herself. A sense of pride washed over her. She'd overcome everything that was thrown at her and came out the other side alive.

Philip was sitting beside her bed when she opened the door. As soon as he saw her, he leaped up. "Erin, oh my God." His eyes widened as he looked her over.

She didn't respond. Instead, she lowered her head and dragged herself towards the bed, knowing he'd watch her every move. Refusing to look at him, she continued on, and was almost to the bed when he came to her aid. Too late.

"What happened up there, babe?" he asked, stroking her hair off her sweaty forehead.

She moved her head away from his hand and made direct eye contact. "You left me."

"What? I went to get help, babe. I didn't know the storm was going to swoop in that—"

"You left me!" she snapped. As soon as the words left her mouth, tears brimmed—visuals of her ordeal back in her mind.

Philip remained silent, leaning into her instead, hugging her to him.

Her emotions took over then, the tears dripping from her nose and chin. For the next hour or so, she stayed in his silent embrace, hating him for what he'd done, but unable to break away from the comfort of his arms.

The night nurse, Linda Barkley, who Erin had met the night before, came in to check as part of her rounds. She was a stout lady, who wore her hair in a messy bun—her uniform stretched, struggling to contain her.

Erin had read her straight away, seeing that while she was kind, she had a bulldog personality and wasn't the type you talked back to. This didn't stop Phil putting it up to her when he was asked to go home for the night and return during visiting hours, as per hospital policy.

He looked her up and down, and Erin could see that he was judging the woman on her appearance, scoffing at her rotund face. Next thing, he leaned in and simply but firmly told her he was staying the night with his fiancé. His lack of aggression and calm assertiveness surprised Erin. She didn't argue—too exhausted and lonely.

Nurse Barkley left in a huff.

It was the early hours of the morning and Erin was beginning to perk up, possibly a result of the anaesthetic wearing off, allowing her to think clearer.

"Where's my dad?" she asked.

"I spoke to him earlier, told him I'd be here for the night. He said he'd get here first thing in the morning." He went on to tell her about how he was unable to get back to the car because the police and the park rangers had forced road closures all around the valley.

He shrugged. "The snowfall was the worst on record, babe. There was nothing I could do."

She stared at him, and he averted his gaze and looked to be lost in his own thoughts. Had to be the guilt. A little voice in the back of her head niggled at her until she listened, and agreed—his excuse of an apology lacked any real sincerity.

"Where did you go?" she asked.

He explained that he had no choice but to

shelter in a guesthouse and wait out the storm, and was going to go back up as soon as it passed, but then got a call from the hospital.

Not a chance was she believing that—it just didn't sit right—but she was in no state to argue or even raise her voice. The last thing she needed was one of his temper flare-ups, and with the painkillers wearing off, all she wanted now was to see her baby, who she realised Phil hadn't once mentioned. He convinced her to remain in the bed, and she was too weak to do anything but obey.

As the night went on, it became clear that Nurse Barkley was the only one left on duty, sitting at the station in the corridor. She'd administered painkillers, telling Erin that she was struggling to get into *one of those Stephen King novels*.

Lights were off, with just the glow from the dimmed corridor their only illumination.

"I'm going to take a piss, babe, and then get some kip here on the chair. Is that okay?" He didn't wait for an answer, making his way over to the toilet.

Erin lay there, staring at the night through the window. Perplexed, she replayed everything over and over. Nothing added up. She didn't know if it was her or Philip, but something was off, and that little voice wouldn't shut up. Whatever it was, she couldn't put her finger on it. Maybe it was the shock or the trauma still overwhelming her, or shades of the delirium she'd slipped into—she didn't know. For fuck's sake, she'd been savaged by a werewolf, and delivered her baby by herself, yet you'd never think anything had happened from Phil's reaction—calm, even distant; definitely less tense than normal. He even moved differently about the place, gliding into the toilet with an easy-going stride, instead of his usual Alpha saunter.

As she lay listening and watching, that little voice in the back of her mind nudged her again. She shifted down the bed to Phil's jacket, obeying the compulsion to rummage through his pockets. She'd never done it before, and there was no rational reason for it now—just an inexplicable urge.

She found nothing out of the ordinary—a set of keys, his wallet, and some loose change. When she opened the wallet, she saw his bank cards and driver's license, as expected, but the picture slot was vacant. It used to house an old photo of the two of them from their second date. The cash compartment contained crumpled receipts. She flicked through them, but nothing struck a chord with her.

The toilet flushed and her heart skipped, but then the sound of water flowing sent a wave of relief through her—at least he remembered to wash his hands. As she fixed everything back into the wallet, she noticed it—that thing her instinct had drawn her to. What she thought was a folded receipt, was in fact an airline boarding pass. A million questions flashed through her as she studied it—a one-way ticket to Canada, with his name on it.

Phil returned and found her shaking, glaring at him.

"You left me," she said, her voice quivering. "On purpose!"

Before he could reply, she held out the boarding pass. "You left me up there. How could you?"

"The rangers closed the roads. I told you..." Then he noticed what was in her hand.

"I can't believe you left me up there. In my state, you should have been there. How could you do this to us? Our baby. Me. How the fuck could you do that?" she cried, her breath coming fast and shallow, her voice echoing off the walls.

Phil's face twitched, his eyes squinting. "You want to know why, huh? Do you?" His jaw muscles bulged with the tension in his words. "I'll tell you why. Because your wonderful father paid me to go."

That hit her like a ton of bricks. She tried to shape the words, but so many ran through her head. "W... What d'you...mean? You're a fucking liar!"

"I mean what I said, Erin. He paid me to leave you."

"And you accepted? Did he pay you to try to kill me?" She couldn't believe the words she was hearing. The reality of it bore down on her with a pressure she'd never experienced in her life.

"No, Erin, that part was on me. I took his money, gladly, but wasn't going to leave without making a *fuck you* statement I'm sure that bitter old prick would appreciate." He almost spat the words out, his tone sadistic. "Him and his fucking dog sanctuary."

He glanced around, then gulped, as if preparing for something big. "Him finding you in there would have been the perfect farewell note." He glared at her, a look she'd seen too often in their apartment. "You weren't supposed to come out of it, you fucking bitch!"

She held her face, wet with tears. "Please, Phil, tell me this isn't true. Tell me it's lies."

He shrugged, held his shoulders high. "Sorry, Erin, it was a sloppy plan, but if I can't be with you, then no one can."

Within seconds, the transformation that washed over him was complete. The monster she knew so well had returned, but this time with murder in his eyes. His face flushed, boiling with rage. His eyes zoned in on her with a stone-cold killer glare.

He lunged at her and grabbed her shoulders, pinning her to the bed, glaring at her with a frenzied madness that reminded her of the wolf.

"Why didn't you stay up there, huh? Why didn't you just fucking die?'"

She tried to move, but he was too strong. "What about your son? What about our child?"

"Fuck the child! I told you, I'm sick of it all. I hated my life with you and that hole we lived in. I told you so many times, but you never listened, always coming back with shite like *we'll get through it*. And don't think I don't know what you meant by that. Ask your fucking daddy to bail us out, huh? Isn't that it?"

It spewed out of him, a flood of hatred, obviously bottled up and festering for months, if not years. He pushed harder on her shoulders.

"You're hurting me!"

"I wanted that job in Canada and all you did was hold me back. I'm sick of you and him ruining my life."

"Then go!" she snapped, squirming under him, unable to move. "Don't...let us...burden you."

"That baby probably isn't even mine, anyway. No doubt your fucking daddy would be all over him and I'd never get a look in. Joseph Greene and his fucking *empire*."

"Go then! Fuck off to Canada, but you'll be on your own."

He frowned at her. "What are you on about?"

"Your mate, Geoff? Well, he won't be there to lick your arse. Oh, no, poor Geoff is lying up there in the valley. You wanted me gone, you bastard, well fuck you, I ended that slimy prick."

His eyes blazed. "Geoff is dead? What're you saying? Geoff isn't here, he's..." He dragged her up and glared at her. "What are you saying, you fucking bitch!"

"He's dead!" she screamed. "I stabbed the bastard in the neck, when he was a wolf."

"What the fuck are you on about?" His eyes scanned hers, flicking from left to right. "Geoff's not here. He's... He's—"

"Dead!" she spat, relishing the confusion in his eyes.

"No! You're insane." In a flash, he whipped the pillow out from under her and pressed it over her face, his immense weight crushing her into the mattress.

She struggled with every ounce of energy she had left in her body, but it was no use, the red mist controlled Phil and she didn't have the physical strength to repel it.

His was saying something, but his words were muffled through the pillow. She thought she caught "die up there", but she wasn't sure, focused as she was on trying to free herself and not releasing her last breath, now burning in her lungs.

The force being applied to her face was crushing, and even though she wanted to scream, she knew that would release any remaining oxygen. The realisation that her body was shutting down sparked an animal instinct reminiscent of that which drove her to defeat the wolf in the mountains. She gritted her teeth and clawed at his arms for all she was worth. As she struggled, she became aware that something was coursing through her veins— adrenaline-like, but different—something she couldn't pinpoint, but her strength was definitely returning.

Then something pricked her arm. The needle? As she pushed against Phil, she visualised her IV port coming loose. She reached across her chest, scraping his skin while sliding beneath him, yanked the needle free, then, with her new surge in strength, jabbed it up in a roundhouse movement she'd seen many times in movies he'd forced her to watch. She connected and the effect was immediate—the pressure lifting from her face and body.

The gawping inhalation nearly burst her lungs it was so fierce, but the relief was enormous. She flung the pillow off the bed, coughing and gagging as she searched the room for Phil. He stood there, over at the opposite bed, his hand covering the side of his neck, his face white, as if he'd seen a ghost. Blood seeped out between his fingers. She must have hit the mark.

A murderous rage she'd never seen before radiated from him—his brows down, his eyes locking on her—morphing into pure-psycho mode. He ran towards her, eating the distance between them in what felt like a split-second. When his hands locked onto her throat, her instincts kicked in and she grabbed the glass of water from the bedside locker, then growled as she smashed it into the side of his face. It shattered and he shot back, blood pouring from the wound.

He roared as he used both hands to cover his neck and face, then groaned and cursed as he picked shards of glass from his shredded cheek.

"My face! My face!"

Erin rolled off the side of the bed and dragged her leg behind her, trying to create distance, but there was nowhere to go with him between her and the ward entrance.

"Help!" she screamed. "Help!"

"What's going on in here?" Nurse Barkley shouted as she stormed onto the ward, the lights flicking on. Her eyes widened at the sight that met her. "Security! Security!"

Phil grabbed his jacket from the bed and dashed for the door, but the nurse took the brave option and blocked his exit, standing in the middle of the doorway, both arms out.

"Get the fuck out of my way, woman."

"Not on my watch, Mister. Just what the hell is going on here?" She looked past him to Erin.

"He tried to kill me. Twice!"

"What?" she blurted out, looking from her to Phil and back again, as if she wasn't sure who had made the accusation.

"I'm telling you," Erin screamed. "He brought me up the mountains to that wolf sanctuary and left me there to be savaged."

Phil grabbed hold of the nurse's waist and dragged her away from the doorway. The woman slammed into the wall and slid to the floor, obviously dazed. Phil climbed on top of her and pressed her face into the floor with his knee, holding a shard of glass to her throat, blood dripping onto her head from his gushing wounds.

"Security will be here any second," she screeched. "Security! Sec—" But she never got to finish, her face smashing into the floor with a thump that nearly had Erin puking.

Phil looked up at her, his glare venomous.

"Jesus, Christ, Philip, what have you done to her?"

"Fuck her. Fuck you all. Why didn't you just die?"

Her mouth fell open, but no words came.

Doors crashed open out in the corridor. Phil flinched and got to his feet. He pointed at Erin and stepped towards her, but stopped and opted to head for the exit instead, picking his jacket up on his way. He looked back at her, took a deep breath, then turned to the doorway.

As soon as the security guard stepped through, the shard of glass was shoved into his face. Erin screamed. The guy was an old man, and he fell to the ground clutching his face. Phil, bleeding profusely, glanced back at her before sprinting out of the ward and down the corridor. A door slammed and alarms rang, and she knew he'd escaped into the darkness of the night.

SIXTEEN

Six months had passed—six full moons—since the child's frenetic entrance into this world. Erin's recovery was complete. She could walk now without the use of a crutch or cane, and her doctors had been nothing less than amazed at her rapid recovery. But they didn't know about the lycan blood teeming its way through her veins. Yet while her visible wounds were healed, beneath the surface many scars remained—scars that would always remind her of the day her life changed forever, the day she went down to hell and looked her demons in the eye. On that day, she overcame everything thrown at her. She'd faced the ultimate test and could now hold her head high.

"Another drink, love?" Joseph Greene asked, his raspy voice interrupting her thoughts. These days, she spent most of her time at the family holiday home by Lough Drumard, just outside the countryside town of Oghill, another plot of land her father owned. The rear veranda overlooked an absolute majesty of still, clear water and forested hills.

Those hills beyond the lake met the early-evening sky, creating a summer backdrop that many holiday-home owners spent the season admiring and painting. The landscape, covered in forest and full of wildlife, was nothing less than breathtaking. Erin looked up and smiled. "Sure. Thanks, Daddy."

He poured red wine into the glass parked beside her deckchair.

Baby Toby slept soundly in the family Silver Cross pram, its stainless-steel frame still as strong as the day it was brought home, four generations ago from a market somewhere in Dublin City.

She glanced up and caught the look of affection in her father's eyes.

"Your mother would've loved this," he said, sitting into his chair. "She loved it up here."

"I know, Daddy. She always liked the peace and quiet."

He sipped his wine and leaned forward. "My life was way too busy for her. I never appreciated our time together." He shook his head in a sad, slow movement. "I just didn't see all of this coming. But, bless her, she gave me this exceptional gift." He rolled up his sleeve, revealing scarring in the shape of a bite mark. Then, he swirled his wine and held it to his nose, closed his eyes, and sniffed. "Best kiss she ever gave me. Bliss."

Something banged around the front of the house, but it evoked no shock from either of them. Every knock at their door was expected, with uninvited visitors rarely calling. This would be a delivery of tomorrow's first print, so Joseph Greene could stay ahead of his rivals in a business world that took no prisoners. It was the only sidestep he took from his off-the-grid existence here in the Cavan lakes, where no mobile phones or computers were tolerated.

"I'll grab it." he said, springing out of the chair with a youthful exuberance—a display of vigour unexpected for a man of his age.

Erin smiled at his confident walk—the same energy flowed through her body as the next full moon drew near. She took a deep breath of clean evening air and leaned over to look in the pram. Toby was tucked under a blue, knitted blanket, and slept with a cheeky smirk on his face.

Dusk sent its golden rays across the lake, the last beads of daylight preparing to slip behind the hills. It was always around this time that she would look at him and shed a tear. Little Toby had the look of his father—something that hurt her to the core. Philip. She still loved him, but not like before, and it helped to take time out to focus on his horrible deeds, even if harking back to that time kept her hooked to the past.

She was sure it would all pass, in time.

Joseph returned with the newspaper tucked under his arm and a fresh bottle of wine in hand. He pointed to the label, but Erin wasn't interested in what vineyard it came from. Italy, France, South Africa, it didn't matter to her.

He returned to his chair. "Now, let's see what tomorrow has to offer." He opened the paper and snapped it into shape, a sound she remembered well from her childhood. There were always newspapers, usually open at the business page.

She stared at the darkening sky. Another day was nearing its end, with the light leaving the land.

Something on the far side of the lake caught her attention. The hairs on her forearms prickled as she squinted, not sure she was seeing it. In the distance, a pack of wolves moved along the treeline—what looked to be three adults and four cubs making their way to the water.

Her stomach lurched and the hairs shot up on the back of her neck. A daydream, surely?

She honed in on them, seeing their thick, grey fur ruffle in the breeze rolling down the hill. After her initial reaction, she realised she wasn't afraid. They weren't here for her or her baby. Once they lapped up their fill from the lake, they disappeared into the trees.

"Beautiful, aren't they?" Joseph said, his eyebrows raised, nose twitching—as if he could smell them. "It's the closest I've ever seen them to the lake."

Erin didn't reply, not sure he was seeing the same as her.

"You know they call me that in the boardroom, don't you?"

She looked at him. "What?"

"The Wolf." He sat up, chest out, proud as punch. "You do know it was a *were* that killed your mother, don't you?"

Erin said nothing, not sure what to share with her father, deciding to allow him continue.

"A werewolf," he clarified, just in case she misheard him. "I never did manage to track the fucker down. But I suppose that's the paradox, isn't it? He took her away from me, but also gave me life and the strength to live it the way I want. Heavy lies the crown, so to speak."

The *truth* about her mother's death hit Erin hard, especially after her own wolf experience. Still, it took time to sink into the depths of her heart. And once it reached the point of realisation, she wanted to burst into tears at the thought of her mother's demise. But she held it together, a new skill she'd been learning to master.

"What do you mean, Dad? Tell me."

"Isn't it obvious, darling? This gift is the gift of eternal power. One bite or tear and they can become like us. I've been giving it much thought since your...misadventure in the mountains. Maybe it's time I used it to create my pack. My legacy. Our dynasty."

Inside, she shook her head, but outside she remained still. She understood his desire to be the best—the Alpha in him willing him on to dominate. It was something she'd become used to from her childhood. She kissed Toby on the forehead, then turned to give her father the same.

Joseph looked at her with delight, obviously taking her silence and kiss as agreement. "I think a little piece of me rubbed off on you. I'm glad it did, because without it, you wouldn't be here and we wouldn't have this little man to continue the legacy."

She stared at him for several seconds, then rubbed her calf, a comforting habit she'd adopted over the months. "Perhaps, but I'm just a...mongrel." She looked across the lake again to the empty shore. Had they been there at all?

Her father's snoring made her chuckle. The man fell asleep so easily when he was away from work, especially after a glass or two of wine. The sound brought childhood memories flooding back.

Then she wondered if he'd even spoken just now, or had he been asleep all along? It didn't matter. She sighed, remembering when she would stuff her colouring pencils up his nose while he snored, to get him to jolt awake from the fright.

As she leaned over to move his glass of wine away from his arm, she noticed a small heading in the newspaper he still clutched: *Wolfman still at large!*

She whipped the paper from her father's hands, giving him the same kind of fright he used to get when a pencil was shoved up his nose. Only she didn't laugh this time, shushing him like she did Toby until he fell back to sleep. "Maybe you have rubbed off on me, Daddy, but I killed a wolf, and that was all me, without the gift."

The article was listed in the Bizarre World section, next to the Classifieds:

WOLFMAN STILL AT LARGE!

The incident occurred last weekend on the banks of the Nass River, in the British Columbian wilderness. Witnesses reported that a troop of boy scouts were attacked by what eye witnesses are calling a "Wolfman".

Scoutmaster, Peter Trembley, said he saw the beast attacking one of the boys, and as it tried to drag him off into the woods, Trembley opened fire with his rifle.

"I'm pretty sure I hit it twice. It dropped the kid and scurried off into the dark, but not before stopping to take a good long stare at me. I froze with fear. Never seen anything like it before. Them eyes. We've encountered bears and wolves out here before and managed to scare them off, but this thing was desperate, hungry, and had a pain behind its eyes. I had no choice but to reload and fire again."

Following on from the interview with Mr Trembley, investigators on the scene found unusual trails which included human footprints mixed in with others from a larger beast. It is unclear if this is a hoax gone wrong or a genuine Big Foot case. Peter went on to describe the creature:

"It was huge. A towering six-foot-six easy. Covered in black and grey hair. Although it was slightly bald on top, I knew this from the full moon's reflection that bounced of it."

Also found at the scene were the remains of what appears to be a shredded passport from an Irish national. It is unclear who or what attacked the camp

*that night, but the area is now on red alert and all
camping is prohibited until further notice.*
  – Gillian Robinson, *Bizarre World, Vancouver.*

Erin swallowed hard. What the hell? She
lifted her glass of wine and emptied it in one go.
Then she re-read the article numerous times
while trying to make sense of it.

The stars were coming out, reflecting off the
still lake—the hills behind blurring as darkness
became their master. Now she couldn't tell
where the water ended and the sky began.

She walked to the water's edge and stood
beneath the beautiful night-time canopy.
The article was in her hand, torn from the
newspaper. She crumpled it up and clenched it
in an angry fist. The cool breeze drifting across
the lake brought goosebumps up all over her
body. Or was it the breeze? She took a deep
breath. Time to bring Toby in.

Before she turned, something on the far side
of the lake caught her attention. In her mind's
eye, she knew it couldn't be real—no way could
she see such detail without light. The wolf—a
dominant male—its grey fur shimmering at
the water's edge, helping her define the line
between the reflective world and that above it.

The animal stood still and silent, staring back.

Her mind took her back to when she and
Philip were on holiday in Portugal a couple

of summers ago, and his speech one night over a candlelit dinner about how family was everything to him, and how he'd do anything for her. Was she to blame for not giving him the one thing he asked for? Was she really to blame? She'd produced a child, by herself, in dire conditions. She'd held up her side of the contract, if there'd ever been one. No, she wasn't to blame. She'd been betrayed, and not just by her baby's father.

She picked up a rock by her foot. It was cool to touch, and smooth. She wrapped it with the piece of newspaper, squeezed it hard with both hands, then drew back and threw it as hard as she could out into the mirrored world before her.

The splash was minimal, but the wolf flinched. The rest of the pack had joined him and they all looked at her, their eyes glowing gold in the darkness. Then they turned and disappeared into the night.

The rock took the article into the depths, and with it all her inner turmoil. She wiped a tear from her eye, smiled, then made her way back to the veranda—her mind finally clear.

She studied her father as he dozed in the chair—his snoring rumbling through her. I've killed one wolf before, Daddy, and he was trying to end me. How hard could it be to do it to one while he slept? I'm here to remind you, dear Father, that the next full moon is almost upon us, and you raised a princess who turned into a warrior, and sometimes in business hard decisions have to be made in order to progress.

Then she sat back into her chair and took in all the stars above—uncharted territory, like her darkest thoughts, scary but intriguing. Embracing death wasn't the big fear everyone made it out to be. What terrified her more was the thought of his heart out there, in the big black nothing, no longer beating for her.

THE END

ACKNOWLEDGEMENTS

The forces that come together to turn the hint of an idea into a debut novella are considerable, and something I marvel at every day. Here are a few of the many people that made this book possible:

First of all, I'd like to apologise to John Mulvaney for asking him to endure chapters from my first draft. They were so poorly written. Despite this, he offered a lot of advice and detailed notes, and without him, you would not be holding this book in your hand right now, so I am forever grateful. Thank you.

The Mongrel was born from an idea that came to me while out on a Sunday drive. The fuel gauge was broken in my car and I never noticed that the tank was empty – which almost left me stranded outside Drogheda. From this incident, I managed to put down the first draft of this story. Like all first drafts, the writing was rough and the plot was far from solid. I then got in touch with Eamon Ó Cléirigh at Clear-View Fiction Editing. Eamon is a damned good editor, who spent a lot of time on this book, but to me, he was so much more than that. Without his guidance, input, and attention to detail, I would have never reached the finish line.

Writing was something I always wanted to do, but never pursued seriously. So, when I received my first edits back, I needed to get notes from other writers. I spent the last decade playing bass in various metal bands and through that scene, I met a horror writer from Denmark by the name of Bo Sejer. Bo read my work and offered some excellent advice which made me believe that I could actually publish this book, someday.

Social Media became a big part of promoting this book, and through that, I feel fortunate to have conversed with some really talented and established writers. I'd like to thank Adam Nevill, Matt Hayward, Tim Lebbon, and Ted E. Grau for their valuable advice, time, and well wishes. They didn't have to respond or indulge me, but they did and it acted as an inspiration that helped me plough through the tough days when the blank page was kicking my arse.

I'd like to thank everyone at Matador Publishing who assisted with the publishing of this book. To Hannah Dakin and Joe Shillito especially for their efforts and ability to turn my idea into this book. Not to mention putting up with every little request and question I had.

A special thanks to Sarah Brophy, the artist who painted the book cover. She is an amazing talent, who captured the essence of this book perfectly.

My penultimate thanks go to Barry Keegan. Barry has supported my creative efforts from day one and without his support, advice, and everything else in between, there is no way I'd have the self-belief to pursue the craft of writing. Thank you, man!

Finally, I'd like to thank my family for enduring the countless nights I spent in front of my laptop. Without your patience, love, and support, I simply would not exist. Orla and Samuel are my life, my home, my love, and my everything.

ABOUT THE AUTHOR

Seán O'Connor was born in 1985, and grew up at the foot of the Dublin Mountains. From a young age he became fascinated with fiction, particularly stories based on the supernatural, horror, and the darker side of the human psyche.

He currently resides in Fingal County on the north side of Dublin, with his Fiancée and son, where he is at work on his next tale of woe.